The Little Orphan's Christmas Miracle

NELL HARTE

©Copyright 2022 Nell Harte

All Rights Reserved

License Notes

This Book is licensed for personal enjoyment only. It may not be resold. No part of this work may be reproduced in any form or by any electronic or mechanical means including information storage and retrieval systems, without written permission from the author.

Disclaimer

This story is a work of fiction, any resemblance to people is purely coincidence. All places, names, events, businesses, etc. are used in a fictional manner. All characters are from the imagination of the author.

Table of Contents

Part One 1

   Chapter One 3

   Chapter Two 13

   Chapter Three 27

   Chapter Four 41

Part Two 62

   Chapter Five 63

   Chapter Six. 85

   Chapter Seven 99

Part Three 117

   Chapter Eight 119

   Chapter Nine 133

   Chapter Ten 145

Part Four 156

   Chapter Eleven 157

   Chapter Twelve 171

Epilogue 191

Subscribe here to receive Nell Harte's newsletter 194

PREVIEW *195*

    The Nurses Plight 197

    Chapter One 199

Part One

Chapter One

London

1852

The carollers had all gone home, the Christmas Eve dinners had all been eaten, the wreaths had all been frozen stiff on the doorways, the Nativity scenes were all slumbering in dark living rooms, the sun had been gone for a very long time, the kisses had been exchanged under the mistletoe, and the whole city of London had fallen dark and silent as though it was any other morning.

The grand new clock tower that people called Big Ben tolled out four long, sonorous notes. Its sound was almost the only sound in the entire city, except for the shriek of the wind around corners and under eaves, rattling every one of the small, squinting windows of the workhouse.

Even on a street as poor as this one, Christmas could still be found. The church on the corner was all lit up with candles, every surface bedecked in ribbons and holly, great drapes of mistletoe hanging on the backs of every pew.

It seemed as though the day's carols still hung somewhere in the rafters of the church. Up and down and across the street, too, stockings hung on mantelpieces and wreaths bumped and crunched on doors, every leaf edged with a pure white border of frost.

But in the workhouse itself, deep inside its dank halls, hiding in the women's dormitory that at that moment echoed with screams, in the heart of the old matron crouched at the foot of one of the narrow beds, Christmas was something that had perished a long, long time ago.

"Stop your noise, girl," growled Rosalyn West. "You'll wake the whole house."

In response, the girl that sat on the bed with her knees drawn up to her chest let out a long, keening moan against gritted teeth. A slip of a girl, she was. Her shoulders jutted hopelessly against the rough cloth of her white nightgown. Her cheeks were scarlet, sweat trickling down them as she panted. How old was she? Sixteen? Seventeen? If that.

Mrs. West pulled back the hem of the nightgown for a better view. "The baby's crowning. You'll need to push soon."

"I can't," sobbed the girl. She fell back against the pillows, her fingertips white where they clutched her legs just below the knees. "I can't push anymore."

Mrs, West resisted the urge to rub her burning eyes. "We don't want to be here all night," she barked.

The girl raised her weary head and looked around at the silent audience that surrounded her. Every woman in the workhouse was staring. She glanced at Mrs. West's face, as though to ask for a little privacy, but then another long, shuddering contraction gripped her body, making her curl in half and let out a primal shriek.

"Push. Push!" barked Mrs. West.

The girl's scream rose to an inhuman pitch, her toes curling deep into the straw mattress, and a rush of fluid gushed over the bed. The babe's face appeared, scrunched up, purple and blue. Perhaps it would be dead. It would be better, in a way, if the child was dead.

The mother was sobbing. "I can't. I can't. I have no strength left." Her fingers were starting to go limp.

"You can't give up now," Mrs. West ordered. "One more push. One more *good* push."

"No. No, I don't have it in me." The girl's tears mingled with sweat and soaked into her nightgown. "Make it stop. Please, please, please, make it stop." Her sobs were desperate and childlike now. Begging.

Mrs. West glared at the girl. What was her name? It took her a few moments to remember. Joanna. Joanna Gray.

"Joanna," she snapped. "Open your eyes."

Joanna did so, more out of the long habit of dreading obedience than anything else.

"You shall push. Now." Mrs. West reached for a towel and held it out, ready. "Or you and your child will both be dead before the hour is out."

Joanna's eyes widened in terror. Another contraction washed through her body, and she threw back her head and screamed, a raw and hoarse and despairing sound, and her entire body curled. The baby was shooting towards Mrs. West then, a rush of blood and fluid and purplish skin.

She caught it, wrapped the blanket around it and lifted it from the soaked bedclothes.

Joanna fell back, her limp arms collapsing on either side of the narrow bed, and for a moment Mrs. West was certain the girl was dead.

It was at that moment that a feeble cry rose from the bundle in her arms. She looked down to see that the babe was not dead after all. Tiny fists were outstretched on arms thinner than a man's fingers, and the little mouth was wide open, colour flushing into the baby's face as it screamed, drawing frigid air into tiny lungs for the first time.

For a few seconds, Mrs. West felt something other than the chaos of roaring pain that had been tearing her apart for so very long. At that moment she was no longer an exhausted and angry widow crouched on a cold workhouse floor, holding a baby that no one had planned and nobody wanted.

She was a young mother herself, although not as young as this one, sitting up in a warm and clean bed, holding in her arms a baby that she had longed for since she could remember. She looked down not into the face of this emaciated, undersized baby, but into the face of the baby she herself had prayed for, for so many years.

And she was not in a great workhouse dormitory surrounded by desperate women, but in a bedroom with a midwife washing her hands in the corner and, beside her, a man whose eyes were filled with love and pride.

Then, Joanna Gray sat up, sucking in a long and desperate breath, clawing her way back to life. She reached out, her pale eyes crazed, as though the sound of that cry had awakened her from the brink of death. "Give it to me," she croaked. "Give it."

Mrs. West looked into the girl's eyes and saw not maternal love but a fierce, base instinct clawing to the surface. She held out the baby, and the girl grabbed it awkwardly, and as it was lifted from Mrs. West's arms, it was as though it was all happening again.

Driving home from church that Sunday, laughing together. Little Miss West's eyes round and bright. Mr. West at the reins, his smile wide. The out-of-control brewers' dray barrelling around the corner. There had been splintering wood, screaming, and a terrible, terrible silence. A silence that followed widowed, childless Mrs. West into this very room, into the centre of her very heart.

Mrs. West did not scream or cry. There was no point. She had screamed and cried until it seemed her very spirit had been poured out of her along with her voice. She cut the cord, covered up the new mother, wrapped a clean towel around the baby.

She moved Joanna and the child onto the next bed and stripped the soiled one. She stood over them both, amazed that they were alive, this young woman whose ribs showed plainly under her skin as she fed the baby, this infant whose fingers and toes were blue already with the pervasive cold that seeped into the stones of the warehouse.

How was it that these two were alive, when her dear John and her sweet Anna were dead?

Joanna closed her eyes and leaned her head back against the pillow, her arms limp around the baby.

"What's the child's name?" Mrs. West asked.

Joanna's eyes opened. "What?"

"You have to name the child. I must write it down in the ledger and arrange for the christening." Mrs. West snorted a little, looking away at that last word. As if this wretch deserved such grace. The irony that she herself deserved no grace, that perhaps nobody did, that perhaps that was the very nature of grace, did not occur to her.

"Oh, I... I..." Joanna looked down, parted the blankets slightly. "A girl," she breathed. "A little girl." She stared down at the baby as though it was the whole world.

"A name," snapped Mrs. West.

Joanna raised fevered eyes upon the world and gazed through the one tiny window of the room. The church was just visible, all lit up with candlelight, a wreath hanging from the door.

"It's Christmas," she said, surprised.

"Yes." Mrs. West folded her arms.

Joanna was silent for a long moment, staring at the baby. "I have no family name to give you," she whispered, tracing a finger along the tiny cheek. "So let's name you something happy. Something Christmassy."

Mrs. West waited without patience.

"Holly." Joanna looked up. "Holly Gray. That's my baby's name."

Mrs. West nodded briefly and turned to leave.

Let's name you something happy.

A pathetic attempt, she thought, at believing that Christmas meant anything and that this little girl's life would be anything but misery.

* * * *

Mrs. West had slept barely an hour when she had to rise again, wake the inmates, bully the staff into getting their breakfast ready, and start the day. A day like any other, until she flung wide the workhouse door and heard the lively sound of the church choir singing "Joy to the World" in the church next door. The sound sickened her. What joy was there in this world, she wondered, looking up and down the bleak and grey street? What joy was there in a world that could take everything from you in one heartbeat, in one collision, in one fell swoop?

She was the one who had wanted to take that route home from church that morning.

The wind was freezing. She was grateful for its howl in her ears as she walked down the short path to the gate of the workhouse grounds; it drowned out some of the Christmas carol. She unlocked the gate with a giant key on a heavy iron ring, but before she could turn back into the workhouse, a voice reached her ears.

"Hallooo, Mrs. West! Wait!"

She looked up. The familiar figure of a cheerful, portly policeman was strutting up the street towards her, and she groaned inwardly. The last thing she wanted to do this morning was to deal with happy people.

Happiness grated on her pain, like salt in a wound. And Constable Joey Mitchell was one of the happiest people she knew. His jolly red cheeks were, as always, squashed by a wide smile; a tumult of golden curls peeked out from under his hat, and, to her immense disgust, he was towing a very small boy along by the arm.

The boy was one of the scruffiest children that Mrs. West had ever seen, and she had seen a good many scruffy children. The tiny bones in his thin arms jutted against pale skin stretched tight over his frame, as though he had nothing to spare, not even skin.

His eyes were deeply buried in great hollows in his face, and they were a brown so dark they were almost completely black, like great pits of need staring up at her. Though he could not have been more than three years old, his black hair hung in awful mats, reaching just beneath his chin.

An oversized shirt hung from his bony frame, covered with holes, and his tiny feet were bare. He had two toes missing on each foot, the little toe and the one beside it. Frostbite, Mrs. West knew, without having to ask; some of the skin was still blackened. She wondered how he had survived this long.

"Found this little chap wanderin' around all on his own, like," bubbled the constable. "Told him you'd take good care of him, didn't I, little man?"

The boy regarded them both speechlessly. His tears were washing down his neck, black with dirt.

"Good morning, constable," said Mrs. West stiffly. "Where did you find him?"

"Oh, down by the slums, poor mite. Scratchin' around in the rubbish for something to eat." Joey beamed at her. "He'll be safe with you."

"I'm afraid so," Mrs. West sighed. "Do you know his name?"

"He says it's Theodore and he can't find his mam. I'd wager he's been abandoned." He ruffled the boys head "Theodore's quite a big name for such a little chap, isn't it?"

The child continued to cry, slowly and continuously, as though he had been crying for as long as he could remember.

"I suppose he has to come in, then," said Mrs. West with distaste. She held open the gate. "Come on."

Theodore hesitated.

"Run along, lad." Joey disentangled his hand from the boy's and gave him a friendly little shove. "Mrs. West will take care of you."

Theodore stared up at her for a long moment. Then, shoulders slumping, he shuffled through the gate.

She slammed it behind him. "Good day to you," she said to Joey.

Joey grinned and doffed his hat. "Merry Christmas, Mrs. West!"

Mrs. West gripped the boy by the arm and marched him up to the workhouse. No day could be merry in which she had two more mouths to feed.

And to Mrs. West, there was no Christmas.

Chapter Two

Four Years Later

A piece of straw was poking into Holly's cheek. She brushed at it, giggling when it tickled across her nose.

"Hush," Mama's voice whispered. A cold hand gripped her arm. "Hush, Holly."

Holly sneezed. She knew it was wrong when Mama had told her to hush, but she couldn't help it.

"Holly!" Mama hissed. "Be quiet."

Holly opened her eyes. Mama's pinched, pale face hovered in front of her. Her own skinny back was pressed against the wall; her head was pillowed on Mama's arm. Mama shifted uncomfortably, and the bed squeaked as the other woman who shared it with them – Rhonda – rolled over. She was bigger than Mama, and shoved her effortlessly against Holly; Mama braced her hands on the wall to keep Holly from getting squashed.

"I'm sorry, Mama," Holly whispered.

"Shhh. Please, poppet. Just go back to sleep," Mama breathed. She hooked a strand of hair out of Holly's face. "It's not morning yet."

Holly obediently closed her eyes and nuzzled against Mama's chest. Mama stroked her hair, which she loved very much. Her tummy was aching with hunger.

"Mama?" she whispered.

"Holly, please." Mama closed her eyes, her head sinking onto the straw. "Just be quiet a little longer."

"All right." Holly paused. "I'm hungry."

"Yes. We all are. But hush now."

It was too late. The bed creaked as Rhonda sat up, her eyes glaring down at Mama and Holly through slitted lids, a red pattern on her cheek where it had been pressed against the straw.

"Silence that brat," she growled, "or I'll do it myself."

"Yes, Rhonda, of course." Mama cowered against Holly, wrapping her in her arms. "I'm sorry. It won't happen again."

"It better not," snarled Rhonda. She sank back onto the straw mattress, giving Mama a cruel thump with her elbow as she did so, not quite by accident.

Holly cuddled against Mama, feeling sorry that she had woken Rhonda, but she couldn't say so because Rhonda would be angry again. She wished people would stop being angry with Mama. Mama was the whole world. With a small finger, she traced the curve of Mama's cheek.

Normally, this would make Mama smile a little bit. Instead, now, she squeezed her eyes shut a little tighter, and a teardrop squeezed out of one eye and ran down her nose.

Mama cried a lot. Holly wished she would smile a little bit more, and she didn't understand why her touch wasn't working like it always did. She cuddled against her body and closed her eyes.

It felt like seconds later that the breakfast bell was clanging and Rhonda was leaping out of bed, elbowing the other women out of the way as they headed for the breakfast hall. Holly sat up, grabbing Mama's hand. "Mama, Mama, wake up!" she said. "It's Christmas! It's Christmas!"

Mama sat up very slowly, tears running down her cheeks. Holly couldn't understand. The other women had been talking about Christmas for weeks. Holly wasn't exactly sure what it was, only that she had a vague memory of excitement from a long time ago, and today everyone was chattering about it. They said that there wouldn't be any work – Mama hated work, even though Holly tried to help – and the women had talked about a special dinner, with enough food for everyone, which Holly hadn't known was a possibility.

Christmas sounded perfect. Why was Mama sad about it?

"Mama, what wrong?" Holly gripped Mama's sleeve and stared up at her.

"Nothing, love." Mama wiped at her tears, then scooped Holly into her arms. "Sit with me just a little while before we wash up and go to breakfast."

Holly squirmed. "But Mama, I'm hungry."

"I know. I know. But just give me two minutes more," Mama breathed. She held Holly against her chest, pressing her nose into Holly's neck and taking a deep breath as though she liked the smell. "Just two minutes more," she whispered.

Holly leaned her head against Mama's shoulder and closed her eyes, wrapping her small fists in the matted locks of her mother's hair. They sat together like that for a few seconds, just breathing. Holly could feel the thud of Mama's heart against her cheek.

The breakfast bell rang again, and Holly sat up. "Mama, I'm hungry!"

"I know, I know." Mama got up and tried to smile, but it was as though her face wasn't quite working right. She gripped Holly's hand. "Come on. Let's go and get breakfast."

They went to the small, frigid washroom, where Mama splashed cold water on Holly's face and tried to clean the tears from her own. Then, following a hallway as long and black as a tunnel, they went through to the dining hall.

"Look, my love." Mama pointed. "All the pretty decorations are for Christmas!"

Holly looked up, a burst of excitement rushed through her. Garlands hung all around the dining hall, punctuated by sprigs of bright holly, their berries brilliantly red. There was a little bunting here and there, too, and when Holly took a deep breath, she smelled something that rarely ever passed her lips: sugar.

Her mouth fell open, and she turned this way and that, staring at it all.

Perhaps the mistletoe was a bit wilted, perhaps the bunting was grubby and hung limp, perhaps the holly berries were rather wrinkled and the sugar was only a few pinches to season the dry porridge they always had for breakfast – but it was new and it was different and Holly could barely remember ever seeing anything new and different in the dining hall before.

"Oh, Mama!" she gasped. "It's pretty!"

Mama was wiping away a tear. "Yes, lovey. It's very pretty."

Holly frowned, reaching up to Mama's cheek. "Mama, why are you crying?"

"Don't worry about that." Mama smiled. "Come on. Let's have some of that porridge."

There was a tiny bit of milk for the porridge, too, and Holly bounced around Mama's knees in excitement as she walked to one of the long thin tables with two tin bowls steaming in her hands. They always sat in the furthest corner of the dining hall, away from the other women, and today was no different. Mama lifted Holly onto a bench as hard as a bone and set the bowl in front of her. "Eat it slowly now, darling," she said. "Or you'll make yourself sick."

She gave Holly a tin spoon. Sniffing with delight at the sweet, creamy scent of this new porridge – she had eaten porridge every morning that she could remember, but could never remember eating it with sugar and milk like this before – she scooped up a spoonful and shoveled it into her mouth. The sweetness burst wonderfully on her tongue.

"Mama!" she cried, mouth full.

"Shhh." Mama stroked her hair. Her own porridge was untouched. "Don't speak with your mouth full."

Holly decided against speaking at all and ate the rest of the porridge in giant gulps, even though Mama kept telling her to slow down. Christmas, she decided, was wonderful. Christmas was bunting in the dining hall and porridge with sugar for breakfast. She was sure she had never had a day as glorious as this before in her life.

When Mama had picked her way through her own oats, she took Holly by the hand and led her up to the front of the dining hall to place their bowls in a huge tin tub. Sometimes Mama and Holly would help with the washing-up, but today it was two other women's turn to do so. They glared sourly at Holly as she stood on tiptoe to place her bowl in the tub. Holly looked up at them, wondering if they even knew it was Christmas. Perhaps she should tell them.

"Merry Christmas," she said.

The stouter of the two women growled and drew back a hand as if to strike her. Holly cringed, but the other woman put a hand on her companion's arm, stopping her.

"Leave the child," she said. "Today it's her birthday you know, she will be four years old." She gave the other woman a meaningful look.

The stouter woman's eyes flickered. She looked away, and Mama tugged on Holly's arm, leading her forward.

"Today's my birthday, Mama?" Holly asked, looking up at her mother.

"Yes, darling." Mama's voice trembled, and when Holly saw where she was staring, she immediately understood why.

Mrs. West was standing in the dining hall doorway.

Holly's stomach seemed to turn a slow somersault inside her belly, making a prickle of cold sweat start on the back of her neck and the palms of her hands. There was nothing in her universe more terrifying than Mrs. West. She was massive, towering over everything, her black eyes lost in the craggy folds of her unforgiving face. Her body looked as hard and immovable as though every part of her had been carved from granite, particularly her jutting lower jaw, and Holly knew from experience that those hands, fastened upon one's ear or applied sharply to one's cheek or buttock, were harder and colder than stone could ever be.

"Gray," Mrs. West growled.

Holly trembled. Gray was the name that Mrs. West always called Mama, although the other women always called her Joanna. Nothing good ever happened when Mrs. West called to Mama.

Mama's hand clenched over Holly's, hard and cold, grinding the small bones in her little hand together.

"Ow," Holly whimpered.

Mama dragged herself before Mrs. West like a prisoner thrown before a merciless judge. "Yes?" she whispered.

"Don't make a fuss now," Mrs. West said shortly. "You know it will do no good. Hand over the child and let's not make it unpleasant."

Mama stood shivering for a long, long moment, and the tears continued to pour down her cheeks. Holly didn't understand. Why was Mama crying? What did *hand over* mean? Was Mrs. West talking about her?

"Mrs. West, please," Mama choked out. "Please."

"You know the rules." Mrs. West held out one hand. "It's this or the streets, Gray."

Mama gripped Holly's hand even tighter. The shock of pain and the sight of Mama's tears made Holly wail, and she felt her own tears burning her eyes.

"She's my baby," Mama said. "She's my baby. Don't take her. You can't take her."

"I think you'll find that I can. You forfeited your right to a family when you came here."

"I was pregnant and starving. I was desperate. There was no other way for her to survive." Mama was sobbing now. "How can you do this? How can you take a child away from her mother?"

Away? Holly let out a shriek, clutching Mama's arm. "Mama! Mama!"

"Enough!" barked Mrs. West. She stepped forward, grabbing Holly's arm. Holly shrieked at the top of her lungs.

"No!" Mama screamed. "No, no, no, no!" Her voice was high and wild now, unnatural, a bird's cry, and her grip on Holly's hand felt like it was going to crush her. But Mrs. West was pulling too now, and she was grabbing Mama's arm and shouting, and the other women were running up to her.

"Let me go!" Mama yelled. Her eyes were wide and wild. "LET ME GO!"

Holly screamed and screamed, her piercing voice ripping through the air, the sound burning her throat. Mama was sobbing, her grip failing, and then Holly's arm shot through Mama's and Mrs. West snatched her up by the arm. The movement wrenched Holly's shoulder, and she shrieked again, but Mrs. West tucked her under her arm and no amount of screaming or pummelling with her wrists could get her free. Two other women had grabbed Mama by the arms, and she was throwing herself against them like a wild animal.

"To the refractory ward with her!" Mrs. West trumpeted.

"No. No. NO!" Mama shrieked.

Holly howled with all of her might, but she was powerless to make any of it stop. She was just a little girl trapped under Mrs. West's iron arm, screaming as her mother was dragged away to the refractory ward, to some place that swallowed her, never to be seen again.

* * * *

Holly screwed her little fists into her eyes. She had cried so much that her whole dress, a ragged little thing made of the ugly striped cloth that all the workhouse children wore, was wet through and clung to her thin shoulders and ribby chest. Her eyes felt as though they had been turned into sandpaper, chafing in their sockets and against her eyelids, but somehow tears were still coursing down her cheeks. She sobbed.

This dormitory, to which Mrs. West had taken her when she was wrenched from Mama's arm, was different to the one where Holly had been with Mama.

It was huge and echoey and the beds were stacked on top of each other in bunks, and where the old dorm had had a single window that looked out over the street and caught the faint glow of a nearby streetlamp and the golden light that always shone through the windows of the church, this room had no windows at all.

In fact, now that the lights had all been turned out throughout the workhouse, it was absolutely and perfectly dark.

The dark made Holly feel like she was not real. All of the things that had defined her world up until that night were gone. There was no window, no streetlamp, no squares of candlelight coming from the church.

There was no warmth from Mama's body tucked around her, no reassuring thud of Mama's heartbeat, no steady pressure of Mama's arm wrapped tightly about her chest. Even the familiar snores of their bed mate were gone. Instead, Holly was lying curled on the corner of a hard little bunk with edges that dug into her ribs, and there were two other little girls on this bunk.

They had bony knees and hard elbows, and when Holly had tried to snuggle up to them, they had used them expediently.

Everything felt like a terrible dream. She felt so small and so cold and so unreal that she might simply come to pieces and blow away on the draft that came in under the dormitory door, as though she had turned to powdery snow.

Her sobs shook her body. They must have shaken the bedframe, too, for one of her companions grasped the soft flesh of her hip between finger and thumb and pinched until Holly squealed.

"Shut up!" hissed the other girl. "Stop your crying! We can't sleep."

"Yes, stop it!" growled a voice from the bunk above her. "Go away!"

Holly sobbed. "Mama! I want Mama!"

"Don't you think we all want our mamas, too?" said the first girl. "Now shut up!"

Holly sobbed all the harder.

"It's no use, Mabel," snapped the girl on the top bunk. "She's going to make this fuss all night."

"Mama!" howled Holly, as though her mother could hear her. "MAMA!"

"That's it!" The top bunk bucked as the big girl on it sat up. "I'm taking her outside."

"But Gwen, we're not allowed outside," gasped the girl beside Holly. "Especially not at night."

"Oh, poo-poo!" snapped Gwen. "I need sleep. And this little brat won't let me have any."

The next moment, a great hand closed over Holly's arm like an iron shackle. Her shriek reached a deafening pitch, then was cut off short as Gwen shook her so hard that her teeth snapped shut upon each other, catching the end of her tongue. Blood flowed into her mouth, and her sobbing only grew louder.

"Well, if you won't learn sense, you'll just have to go," said Gwen. Her grip tightened on Holly's arm, and she was dragged from the bunk and across the cold stone floor to the doorway. She felt and heard, rather than saw, the doorway being wrenched open.

A gust of dreadfully cold air snatched her breath momentarily, and Gwen gave her an almighty shove. Stumbling forward into utter darkness, Holly felt she was sure to plummet over a cliff. Then her outstretched hands slapped against stone. She was in a hallway.

"And stay out," Gwen hissed.

The door slammed. Holly rushed to it, scrabbling at it, sobbing to be let back in again. But the doorknob was too high for her to reach, much too high, and nobody heeded her feeble cries.

Still weeping, Holly stumbled along the hallway, looking for a scrap of warmth or light or anything except for the cold stone floor and the cold stone walls that surrounded her. She held her eyes wide open till they burned, but she saw nothing. Only darkness.

The darkness seemed to be going inside her with every breath, like poison gas, suffocating her. There could have been anything lurking in that darkness. Savage things with long teeth and yellow eyes. Mrs. West, wielding a belt or a cane.

Her exhausted limbs would take her no further, so she sank down with her back to the wall, huddled against the cold stone and crying softly. She covered her face with her hands, feeling the darkness pressing closer and closer, ready to consume her, to crush her.

Something creaked in the dark. Holly squealed, throwing herself down to the floor. What was coming for her? Would it destroy her? Would it kill her with one swipe of foul claws, with one savage snap of a reeking maw?

"Hello," said a small voice.

Trembling head to foot, Holly looked up, her heart still hammering wildly within her chest. Just faintly, she could see the outline of a shadow coming towards her, only this shadow wasn't huge or looming or covered with spikes and teeth. Instead, it was something small and slender, and it was holding out what might have been a hand.

"What's your name?" the small voice asked.

Holly cowered against the wall, but she found the strength to wipe at her sodden cheek. "Holly," she whispered.

"That's a nice name. Christmassy." Small, bony fingers found her hand; she flinched back at first, but their touch was gentle, and they gripped hers.

"I'm scared," Holly whispered.

"Hello, scared," said the voice. "I'm Theodore."

Holly giggled. The boy giggled with her, and sat down next to her. He was a bit bigger than her, but not very much; still, he was warm, and it felt good to be near someone who didn't want to hurt or elbow or beat her or drag her away from her mother.

"I'm all alone," Holly whispered.

The boy nodded. "I know. Me too."

They sat there together in the dark, and Holly stopped crying. And somehow the darkness felt far less penetrating for the presence of Theodore beside her.

Chapter Three

Three Years Later

Holly stayed near the back of the line, careful not to get too close to the bigger girls in front of her. Most importantly, though, she made sure not to stray too far behind. Straying behind would make her stand out; standing out would be sure to catch the attention of Mrs. West.

The matron stood by the long tables at which the children were to help themselves to bowls, spoons, and soup. Her eyes were acid where they rested upon the row of wretched girls waiting for supper. She kept looking up and down the line, her gaze touching the face of each child, as though looking for any sign of joy or relief, ready to stamp it out like an unwelcome flame in a cold, dark night.

Holly shivered, wrapping her arms around her emaciated torso. The hall was as cold as the rest of the workhouse had been all day.

There was a fire in one end, but it sputtered pitifully, succeeding only in providing a little noise and smoke, no real heat. Some of the larger girls had already taken their bowls and gone to sit as close to the fire as possible.

Holly avoided them as much as she could. Grabbing the second-to-last bowl from the pile, she held it up, plugging a small hole in the bottom with one finger.

The server at the big pot of soup gave her a disinterested look and scooped a single ladleful of pale, watery soup into her bowl.

Taking a spoon, Holly clutched it close, sneaking a few bites as she scurried toward the nearest table. It was far from the fire and a terrible draft blew in under the dining hall door, swishing around her ankles, but at least it was unoccupied. Holly threw herself down upon a painfully cold and hard bench and began to suck down her soup as quickly as she could, her spoon splashing in the bowl.

Where small drops were spilled on the table, she quickly mopped them up with her finger and swallowed them down, desperate not to lose a single bite –

"All right, Gray. You know that's mine."

Holly slurped down another two or three mouthfuls before a big hand descended on her and snatched the spoon from her grip. She tried to grab for the bowl, but the other girl ripped it away from her with a laugh that rattled like iron bars.

"You always try to hold onto it, don't you, Gray?" hissed Mabel Griggs.

She slid onto the bench beside Holly, glancing up at Mrs. West, who was busy shouting at a wretched little girl who had dropped her soup. Pushing Holly out of the way, she started to leisurely drink down the rest of the soup. "You know this is mine," she slurred with her mouth full.

"Please." Holly squeezed back tears, tangling her hands in her skirt. "Please, I'm so hungry. Let me have my soup."

"Go ask Mrs. West for more soup." Mabel laughed cruelly.

There was no possibility of that. Holly cast a last, despairing glance at the dregs of soup that Mabel was happily finishing before sliding to the end of the bench and sitting hunched over her aching belly.

Hunger, hunger, hunger.

It had become her companion, the dreaded constant of her dreary life in the workhouse. She had never known anything else. She wanted to cry, but the tears would not come, and so she sat very still instead, trembling a little and wondering why this was her lot.

She had barely ever set foot beyond the workhouse, but she did know that not all little girls spent their days in cold and hunger.

Her eyes wandered across the dining hall to a bony girl sitting slumped over an empty bowl. Leticia Haversham had told her, in a tearful moment when she'd first come to the workhouse, that her family used to have a whole house all their own.

She ate three hot meals every single day and sometimes couldn't finish everything she was given.

What was more, her mama and papa and brother had all lived in the house with her, and they could be together anytime they pleased. It all sounded rather unlikely to Holly. How was it possible for such happiness to exist?

It seemed implausible that such a thing could be in the same world as the intolerable suffering with which she was faced day after day. So she did not stare at Leticia or think about the things she had said, even though she wanted to. She just waited for the bedtime bell to ring, then rose to her feet and blended with the crowd of miserable little girls shuffling to their cold dormitory for another winter night in the workhouse.

Another night being crushed and trampled by Holly's oldest foe: the dark.

* * * *

The kitchen was filled with light. There were so many candles in the small room that not a single shadow dared lurk within it. There were candles on the table, candles on the windowsills, candles on the cabinets, even candles on the mantelpiece above a giant, roaring fire that baked the kitchen as warm as the hottest, sunniest summer day.

It was so warm that Mama was wearing a pretty dress with short, puffy sleeves that showed her smooth white arms. Mama was sitting down on the table, her big eyes sparkling as they rested upon Holly. Holly didn't know what she wanted to stare at the most – Mama, or the piles of bread on the table. Mama's frock looked just like the pretty summer dresses she saw on the churchgoers that went past the dormitory window sometimes on warm Sunday mornings. And she didn't think she'd ever seen that much bread before.

"It's all yours, Holly, darling," said Mama. *Her smile was even brighter than all of the candles, even brighter than the sunlight that came in dazzling shafts through the kitchen window.*

"Mine?" *Holly reached towards her mother, gripping her hand.*

"All yours." *Mama laughed, a tinkling noise.*

"Mama, I love you," *she said.* "I wish I could say it earlier, but now I can."

"Oh, Holly, my darling little pet!" *Mama wrapped her in a hug and smothered her with kisses.* "I love you, too. Now eat your bread."

She pulled off a great fistful of it, lifting it to her face, ready to taste the warm deliciousness. A trail of something grey and runny trickled down her palm. Holly blinked, looking down at it. It was gruel.

Why was the bread filled with gruel?

She looked up. "Mama?"

"Holly!" *Mama screamed. Mrs. West had her! There was a thick rope around her neck, just like the ropes they had picked apart for oakum when Holly was small, and Mrs. West was dragging her out of the house by the rope.* "Holly, no!" *Mama was shrieking.*

"Mama!" Holly rushed forward, and Mrs. West kicked the door open with a guttural cry. Blackness rushed into the cottage, blowing out the candles, leaving just one flickering a little so that Holly could see Mama's face turning blue and then purple as Mrs. West dragged her away into the dark...

"Mama!" Holly screamed, but the faster she ran, the further and further Mama and Mrs. West seemed to be. The darkness was pooling on the floor of the cottage kitchen now, splashing up against the walls; wherever it touched the walls, they melted and collapsed into the rising sea of darkness. Holly was wading, then swimming, screaming and screaming as a wave of darkness splashed over Mama and Mrs. West and they were gone. The darkness was rushing into her nose. Her throat. Her lungs –

Holly sat up with a shriek that ripped through her throat, leaving it raw. Darkness. It was inside her, it was all around her. She screamed and flailed, her hands finding thin blankets, straw mattress, and a furious fist that thudded into her chest.

"Stop it!" hissed the other girl sharing the bed with her. "You'll wake Mabel!"

Holly covered her mouth with her hands, sobs wrenching through her body. Mama had seemed so close. So real.

"Stop it!" snapped the girl, shoving her. "Don't wake her!"

The girl in the bunk beside theirs was stirring now. "Shhh!"

"I can't. I can't." Holly sobbed steadily. "I'm so scared."

"Well, go be scared somewhere else." Her bunkmate grabbed at her dress, trying to shove her out of the bed. "I don't want to get beaten up when you wake Mabel!"

Holly knew she had to stop, knew that Mabel would be on her in a flash if she didn't, but she couldn't. She dragged herself from the bed, weeping, disoriented, the world seemed nothing but darkness around her. Her toe rammed against the foot of the bed, and she squealed.

"Get out of here!" barked one of the girls.

Holly felt her way to the dormitory door in the darkness, pulled it open and stumbled out into the draughty hallway. She sank down in her habitual spot on the cold floor, her sobs still running steadily through her. The world was an abyss all around her. Mama was nowhere.

She was alone, as she was every night, as she had been that appalling night when she had been taken from her mother.

She covered her face with her hands and cried into them, praying for the only relief she ever had from these long, dark nights. And that relief came, finally, some time later, when her bones felt frozen and her eyes were raw from the crying that had still not stopped, in the form of that same quiet voice speaking in the dark.

"Holly?"

She raised her weary head and held out a hand. "Theodore."

Theodore's hand wrapped around hers, and he sat down next to her so that she could lean her head on his shoulder and feel how real he was. Warm and solid and present and real.

"Another bad dream?" Theodore whispered.

"Yes... about Mama." Holly sniffed.

"I'm sorry." Theodore sighed. "I still dream of my mama sometimes, too."

"What do you dream about her?"

"I don't know. Just… her voice. The way her hands felt."

Holly closed her eyes so that she didn't have to see the darkness in the hallway. "You don't remember her, do you?"

"No." Theodore squeezed her hand. "But let's not talk about that now. Did you see the big boxes of mistletoe coming in this afternoon?"

"Mistletoe?" Holly wrapped her arms around her freezing body. "Is it Christmas already?"

"Almost. Tomorrow."

Holly yawned, the smallest stirring of excitement in her belly.

"And it means we'll get something nice for dinner," Theodore added. "Maybe a bit of beef, or even a slice of roast goose."

"Roast goose!" Holly gasped. "Have you ever tasted it?"

"Once, when I was very little. You must have been less than four that year. It was before you came to the girls' dormitory."

"I hope I get to taste it someday."

"I'm sure you will. And tomorrow they'll hang up the mistletoe. It'll all look so much brighter."

"I like mistletoe."

There was a pause, and Theodore chuckled. "I like holly best."

Holly giggled, too, even though it felt strange; she hadn't laughed in such a long time. It was only ever Theodore who could get her to laugh, even if it was only a little.

* * * *

Theodore didn't know how long he sat in the hallway with Holly, but he knew that at times like these, he almost wished the night would never end. It was cold in the hallway and he shivered a little, yet the warmth of Holly's small form curled up by his side seemed to make up for it all.

It was her small, piping voice in his ears and the gentle pressure of her hand in his own that made the hallway seem so much more friendly than the prickly straw mattress in the boys' dormitory. It was so different from the angry voices and rough shoving from the other boys, the curse words that were so prevalent even in the small voices of the littlest boys when they squabbled over food or space on the sleeping pallets. There was nothing kind or soft or gentle in the boys' dormitory. Life was harsh and brutal and messy there.

Life was pointless there.

But here… here, Holly's sobs slowed down when she was curled against his side, and they spoke of softer things, even if they were only dreams. It made Theodore feel a soft warmth in the centre of his chest, like a Christmas candle had been lit there.

He held her hand and sat with her in the dark, and it was the only thing that felt good in his lonely existence.

"Leticia Haversham was telling me about Christmas," Holly said.

"Who's she?" asked Theodore.

"She's new. She had a nice house and a family once. They used to decorate a tree and eat roast chicken and potatoes for Christmas."

"That sounds very nice." Theodore sighed. "Have you ever wondered what it would be like to have a family?"

"I've seen families going to church. Parents with children. They look happy, even if they're quarrelling sometimes."

"I think families must be nice. Even with quarrelling."

"Me too." Holly yawned. "I hope that I can have one, someday."

"So do I," Theodore whispered.

Then, a sound in the darkness. A footstep. Theodore tensed, clutching Holly's hand. She sat up sharply. "What was that?"

"Shhh!" Theodore hissed, but it was too late. Already the clop-clop of footsteps was coming down the hallway towards them, and he saw the dim glow of a candle creeping up the walls.

"Run!" Theodore gasped, scrambling to his feet. "Get back to your dorm!"

"What's going on out there?" roared Mrs. West's voice.

Holly's eyes snapped wide; in the approaching glow of the candle, Theodore saw that her face was pale and grubby, with rivulets of cleanliness where her tears had run. She had mopped at them, smearing dirt and tears over her face. New tears were gathering in them now.

"Go. Go!" Theodore whispered, shoving her. "Get to your dormitory!"

Holly clutched his hand. "Theo – "

"RUN!" Theodore hissed.

Holly gave a hiccupping gasp, turned, and bolted down the hallway, her small feet pattering wildly. Theodore's door was just a few yards away. He lunged for it as the candle came around the corner and brightness filled the hallway. Expecting at any moment a claw to descend upon his collar and drag him to a flogging, Theodore threw himself through the door and shut it quickly, then rushed to his bunk and flung himself inside. The little boys with whom he shared the bunk only muttered in their sleep. He pulled the covers over his head and lay still, his heart hammering, listening.

The door creaked. Light filled the room, and then, the sound of boys stirring. Theodore kept his eyes smoothly shut and breathed very slowly. For an interminable moment, he could feel Mrs. West's eyes crawling through the dormitory like the tentacles of some monster. Then, the light withdrew, and the door closed.

Theodore let out a long breath, curling himself into a ball. Now, he could only pray that Holly had gotten away.

* * * *

Holly was running, her feet slapping on the floor, the hallway bathed in light as the brisk clopping of shoes came after her. The dormitory wasn't far away. Just a few more yards. She stretched her aching legs to their utmost, fleeing with every fibre in her body –

"I have you now!" thundered the dreaded voice of Mrs. West, and an iron claw snapped shut over her arm, almost pulling her off her feet as she was wrenched back.

"No!" Holly's voice was a piercing shriek. "No, no, no!"

"Silence!" Mrs. West shook her with the same force as she had done the day that Holly was taken from her mother.

Holly fell quiet. Perhaps, if she complied with every order this monstrous woman uttered, she would be spared punishment. She closed her eyes, trembling, and prayed for the strength to be still and obedient.

"That's better," said Mrs. West. "Now, what were you doing in the hallway?"

Holly's heart skipped in her chest. *Theodore!* She couldn't let Mrs. West find out that she'd been talking to him.

"Answer me, child," Mrs. West growled. "You know it is forbidden to be out here on your own. Tell me!"

"I was hiding from the dark," Holly whispered. "I had a bad dream and I was trying to hide from the dark. I was so afraid."

Mrs. West's eyes narrowed, deep shadows flickering beneath her stern brow, cast there by the candle she held in one hand. Holly found herself staring at the little flame more than at Mrs. West herself.

"You were talking to someone," the matron said. "I heard you. You were talking to one of the boys." She put her face close to Holly's, hissing the words. "What were you doing?"

"I was talking to myself." Holly dragged her eyes back to the flame. "I was scared and alone and I was talking to myself."

The silence dragged between them, stretching until Holly trembled with the force of it, knowing it would snap at any second. Then Mrs. West turned sharply and strode down the hall, dragging Holly behind her. She was too afraid to ask where they were going, so she hurried after the matron, trying to ignore the tears rolling down her cheeks.

The matron hauled her into the nearest classroom; a bare, cold, windowless room. The flame illuminated scraps of it — small desks, slates, uncomfortable benches, a blackboard — and, crucially, the teacher's desk at the front of the room, and the wooden ruler lying upon it.

"Stand here." Mrs. West yanked her into place in front of the desk.

Holly was sobbing faster now. She knew what was coming; had seen it done to some of the other girls when they misbehaved or, more likely, placed the blame on some other hapless child for their misbehaviour.

Mrs. West gripped the ruler. "Hold out your hand."

Holly swallowed. "Please…"

"Do as you're told!" rapped Mrs. West.

Holly sobbed softly and held out her hand, palm up. It looked very soft and white and helpless in the flickering candle flame.

"Now hold still." Mrs. West raised the ruler.

Holly closed her eyes tightly and turned away, her breath racing in her lungs. A sudden, burning pain burst through her hand, and she cried out.

"I told you to be silent, child." Mrs. West snatched at her burning hand, prying it away from where she had clutched it to her chest. "And don't move."

"Please," Holly sobbed. "Please – "

Mrs. West forced her fingers open, a red welt already throbbing on her palm, and struck her again. This time Holly bit down hard on her lower lip and the small pain distracted her enough that she could keep herself from crying out. Another blow. Another. Just when she felt that the skin could take no more without tearing, Mrs. West let go and tossed the ruler back onto the desk.

"Now go back to bed," she hissed. "And never let me catch you outside the hallway again."

Before Holly could comply, the big woman seized her by the ear, eliciting another scream, and dragged her back down the hallway to the dark, dark dormitory.

Chapter Four

Holly stayed in the middle of the crowd of little girls heading into the dining hall. With her head held low and her aching hand close to her chest, she prayed that no one would see her or notice her. She would have hidden away in bed all day if she had thought that she could get away with it.

But from the moment she stepped into the dining hall, she could feel Mrs. West's eyes upon her, boring into her like drills. Keeping her head down, Holly breathed slowly, trying to hold back the tears that gathered behind her eyes. Her hand ached fiercely; she found it was too sore and swollen for her to unclench her fist.

Walking past Mrs. West on her way to the food table was like tiptoeing by the nose of some sleeping wild beast, ready to tear her limb from limb. She managed it, grabbed a bowl with her good hand, tucked the spoon between two fingers of her sore hand and scurried to the big pot where the usual tasteless gruel was being served.

It was difficult to wolf down a few bites, as was customary, when she stumbled over to the table with one hand too sore to grip either spoon or bowl. She had to wait until she could set down the bowl and sit, seizing the spoon in her good hand, to start gulping down the gruel. Her belly cramped at the speed with which she sucked the food down. It was cold and slid down her throat in a bland, slimy ball, but it was good to have something to eat.

Around her, the mistletoe had already been put up in preparation for the festive day tomorrow. It was a little wilted and cheap, with tattered leaves, and Holly barely spared it a second glance. Some of the girls chattered excitedly, for the hope of some little treat on Christmas day. What did it mean to her? She knew that even if they served beef or goose at Christmas supper, she wouldn't get her fair share of it.

A thump to her shoulder dragged her from her reverie. Mabel was shoving her from the bench. "Move, scrap," she barked, snatching the bowl and spoon from her.

There was no point in fighting. Holly waited, as always, for breakfast time to end, listening to the slurping and smacking of Mabel finishing her breakfast.

At last the girls gathered up in a crowd to take their bowls and spoons for washing-up, and Holly took the bowl that Mabel had emptied and tried to blend with the crowd. All the while, Mrs. West was watching her the way that a wolf would watch some helpless fawn. And though she kept her head down and put not a toe out of line, it felt inevitable when she passed by Mrs. West and the matron reached out and snagged her by the elbow, yanking her out of the group.

"I hope that last night's punishment cleared your memory, child," she hissed.

Holly bit back tears, keeping her hand tightly clenched. "Wh- what do you mean?"

"I mean that I know you were out in that hallway with someone else." Mrs. West leaned close, her breath foul in Holly's face. "And I want to know who it was."

Holly thought of Theodore. When she looked into Mrs. West's face, she saw danger there, and she knew that silence would have consequences. But what would happen if she told Mrs. West who she had been with? Her hand throbbed steadily, giving her an answer. Theodore would suffer the same fate that she had, and she couldn't do that to him. She couldn't bear to think of poor, kind Theodore, the only good thing in her life, being subject to this pain.

"I was alone," she whispered.

Mrs. West's eyes narrowed, her grip on Holly's arm becoming a crushing vice.

"I thought you might say that," she hissed. "Very well. On your own head be it.."

She straightened and began to walk very quickly, dragging Holly with her. Heart pounding, Holly wondered, terrified, if this next punishment would be a beating on the same hand or on the other. What would she do with both hands hurt? But Mrs. West dragged her straight past the classroom and deeper into the dread bowels of the workhouse.

"Where are we going?" Holly gasped, fear lurching in her belly.

Mrs. West cackled. "Where you deserve to be," she said. "The refractory ward."

A memory pierced through Holly's mind, distant and fuzzy and yet still terribly charged with fear. The last time she had seen her mother. People dragging her away. *To the refractory ward with her!* Mrs. West had shouted.

And Holly had never seen her mother again.

"No. No!" she squealed, pulling back. "Don't take me there. Please. Please!"

"Silence!" roared Mrs. West, dragging her inexorably on, and Holly begged and sobbed and screamed and no one came to her aid. She was taken downstairs, deep into the clammy cellar of the workhouse, into a place where mould and cobwebs competed for space in the corners, and finally Mrs. West brought her to a narrow little door in a dark corner.

"No. No, no, no," Holly whispered. "Please. Don't do this." She grabbed at the front of Mrs. West's coat, gripping with all her strength, raising her tear-stained face. "Please don't do this."

Mrs. West didn't meet her eyes. Instead, she pulled the door open and shoved Holly inside. In a panicked moment, Holly saw the room: no windows, a pallet and blankets in one corner, a bucket in the other. The room was no more than three paces long and two paces wide, barely big enough to accommodate the pallet.

"No!" she cried, but Mrs. West slammed the door, sealing her in utter darkness.

Holly screamed. She pounded on the door; she tore at it with her fingernails. But not a sound pierced the darkness of the refractory ward, and no one came looking for her. She screamed until her voice was worn out, and then she sagged down against the door and cried until the tears would no longer come.

Her life had become blackness and terror. She was living her nightmare.

* * * *

Theodore turned onto his other side, carefully, the straw crackling beneath him. Next to him, one of the little boys stirred. "Theo?"

"Shhh." Theodore reached back and gently touched the little boy's shoulder. "Sleep."

There were murmurs of annoyance through the room, and Theodore closed his eyes, willing the other boys to go to sleep. When they all slept, he could sneak out and find Holly. He thought he had heard her voice screaming last night, when Mrs. West had gone down the hall; but when he'd slipped out of bed and opened the door, he hadn't seen or heard anything.

She must have gotten away. Mrs. West must not have seen her. Yet all day, Theodore had worried that Mrs. West had found her and struck her.

He lay very still, listening as the breathing of the other boys slowed and deepened around him. Listening for Holly's soft sobs.

The other boys dropped gradually off to sleep, but no sound of Holly came. Slipping out of bed at last, Theodore padded across the big room in stockinged feet and squeezed out of the door and into the hallway.

The darkness cloaked him, hiding him from prying eyes, and there was no sound. Feeling his way along the wall with one hand, Theodore moved towards the girls' dormitory, daring to raise his voice in a whisper.

"Holly?" he whispered. "Holly, are you out there?"

There was no response. He found their usual spot by the loose brick in the wall nearby and sat down beside it, pulling his knees to his chest and resting his forehead upon them.

If Holly didn't come...

Maybe she was sleeping soundly tonight. She sometimes did. Maybe she was angry with him because of the trouble he had almost caused for her... But no. Holly wouldn't do such a thing. Their friendship was too important... wasn't it?

Or maybe...

The thought was dreadful. Surely even Mrs. West wouldn't be cruel enough to throw such a little child into the refractory ward, would she?

Theodore sagged down onto the floor of the hallway, his arms wrapped around himself, knowing in his heart that Holly had been punished. That was why Mrs. West hadn't come and dragged him from the room; she'd already captured her quarry. What was more, Holly couldn't have told Mrs. West that Theodore had been in the hallway, too. She had stayed quiet for him.

Perhaps she had even been taken to the refractory ward for him.

Theodore covered his face with his small hands and cried. It was unjust, it was appalling, it was horrific – and it was all the more reason why he would do all he could to be kind to sweet little Holly Gray.

* * * *

Holly thought she was dead.

She thought that death must feel a little like this. No one had ever told her what it was like, but people feared it so much that it must be the worst thing in the world, and this was the worst thing she had ever felt.

Her body ached from the pressure of the pallet on her thin, bony limbs. Her hands burned from scratching at the door. The silence pressed down upon her ears like some awesome physical force, and hunger and thirst clawed at her.

How long had she been in here? An hour? A day? A thousand years? There was no time in the refractory ward. There was just darkness and silence.

And then, somehow, incredibly, a sound. Footsteps. Holly raised a head that felt woolly and weary with crying. Her eyes burned; she blinked them open, she thought, although there was no difference whether they were open or closed.

But the footsteps were real, and they were coming nearer. Gripped by both hope and terror, Holly scrambled to her feet and flung herself against the doorway, shrieking. "Let me out! Please! Help me! Help me! Let me go!"

"Silence, child!" rapped the voice of Mrs. West.

Holly's voice died instantly in her throat. She cowered against the back wall of the tiny room, her heart beating broken wings inside her chest. What would the matron do to her next?

There was the sliding of a bolt, the door swung open, and suddenly, gloriously, Holly could see. It was only a dim, grey daylight that reached the basement, and Mrs. West was holding a stub of candle that flickered feebly, diluted by the faint daylight; but it was light, it was real, and she wanted to rush out into it and bask in it and never, ever close her eyes and shut out its glorious presence ever again.

The dark lines of Mrs. West's face and figure were the only things that stopped her. She watched the matron warily, her muscles taut and trembling.

It was Mrs. West who finally spoke, harshly. "I trust that twelve hours in the refractory ward has taught you your lesson, child."

Fear lanced through Holly. What if Mrs. West thought that the lesson wasn't learned at all?

"Yes, ma'am." Holly dropped her eyes, and added, "I'll never, never go outside the dorm at night again."

For a few more appalling seconds, Mrs. West's eyes rested upon her, drilled into her.

"Very well, then," she said at last, stepping back and opening the door. "Breakfast is in. Wash and go to the dining hall at once."

Tears of relief rolled hot down Holly's cheeks. She had to use every ounce of courage she had to walk out of the room instead of running. Mrs. West led her up the stairs and back onto more familiar ground, then to the washroom, where cold and dirty water was waiting for her in a tin basin.

She washed the blood from her torn fingernails and the tears from her face, and then went obediently to the dining hall, and only then did she realize that it was Christmas Day.

There was mistletoe hanging all around the room on long strings erected between bare nails hammered into the walls for that purpose.

The chatter around the long tables and hard benches was a little more lively than usual, and even the servers seemed slightly more cheerful. What was more, they weren't dishing up porridge for the girls. Instead, the heady scent of fried eggs filled the air, and there was something else too: sausages.

Holly had only ever had sausages for supper. Sprigs of holly lay on all of the tables, their bright red berries lending pops of brilliant colour to the dreary room.

"Merry Christmas," said Mrs. West, her words flat and meaningless, and went to scowl at the servers.

Holly plodded forward, held out her plate and accepted a dollop of scrambled eggs and half a gristly sausage. She went to the table and ate the sausage before Mabel could take it. And she did not look at the decorative holly. She did not stare at the mistletoe. She did not taste the sausage.

Instead, her eyes were on the window, a small and cracked thing set in the wall behind the table where the servers stood.

It had a latch on the inside, but no lock. Through it, Holly saw fat flakes of bright white snow coming down softly in front of a grey street, every roof and wall covered in a fine white blanket of snow. And beyond the snow, the wide sweep of the street, and the church with its golden candlelight within, and the song of the people inside just dimly audible from the bleak workhouse interior.

The candles never went out in the church. Even at night, the streetlamps shone.

There were no refractory wards out there and there was no perfect darkness.

Holly sat in silence as Mabel snatched her plate and gulped down the eggs. Disappearing within her imagination, Holly watched the snow falling, and the flicker of the candlelight in the church window.

* * * *

Holly disobeyed Mrs. West's orders that very night.

The hardest part of her plan was staying in bed, completely silent, until all of the other girls fell asleep. It was close to impossible. The darkness was like a great stone upon her chest, crushing her.

The only thing that made her stay still at all was the soft sound of the other girls breathing, and the warmth of the little girls on the bunk beside her, reminding her that she was not completely alone. Lonely, but at least not alone.

When all had grown still around her, Holly crept from the bed and slipped through the door into the hallway, where the faintest light lent scraps of definition to the floors and ceiling. Her heart fluttered in her chest as she followed the curve of the hallway, leading her towards the dining hall. It was a route she walked three times every day and yet by night it seemed alien and unfamiliar. It seemed strange that this would be her last time walking down this hallway.

She reached the door of the boys' dormitory and stopped for a moment, feeling a deep sting in her heart. Perhaps there was still time to say goodbye to Theodore. Perhaps if she opened the door very quietly... Her fingers brushed the doorknob, then stopped, her hand falling once again to her side. No. If they were caught, Theodore would suffer the same fate that she had, and she could not wish the refractory ward upon him. Upon anyone.

Tears stung her eyes, and for a moment she was too afraid to go on. But the fear of staying was worse.

"Goodbye, Theo," she whispered under her breath, then turned and carried on walking to the dining hall.

The door was shut, and Holly felt a desperate pang of fear that it would be locked. But when she reached up and gripped the doorknob, it turned swiftly and silently, and she let herself into the vast room and closed the door as quietly as she could.

At once, Holly turned to the window, and everything seemed better the moment she laid her eyes upon it. There was light out there.

The warm glow of the streetlamp shone down on the pavement; the church was quiet, the doors all locked, but she could see candlelight shimmering through the stained glass, illuminating the wreaths that hung on the doors, bright with holly and dusted with snow.

Her steps were sure now as she strode towards the door. She was wearing both her dresses – she had kept the spare one out of the laundry by hiding it in her pillowcase – and the pair of shoes that had long been a little too small for her. It looked cold outside, but at least it wasn't dark.

The window was stiff and creaked when she tugged at it, the sound echoing horribly around the empty hall. She tugged again, praying no one would hear, and with a dreadful moan, the hinges finally gave way and the window flew open.

The sound reverberated through the workhouse. Immediately, Holly heard a distant shout, and running feet.

Her heart leaped into her mouth. If Mrs. West found her now, she knew that she would be taken back to that refractory ward, and a terrible certainty flooded through her, telling her that she would not survive another stint there.

She could not say exactly what would kill her; she only knew that her time there had been horrifying, and that Mama had gone there and never come back. So she grasped the windowsill with both hands, caught a wild glimpse of the pavement two stories below, hesitated for an instant, heard the bang of the dining hall door flying open, made her choice and flung herself through it.

She had just enough presence of mind to grip the sill for long enough that she fell feet first.

That may have been the end of Holly were it not for the fact that a huge drift of snow had blown up against the workhouse wall. She pitched into it, surrounded instantly by biting cold, her fall broken by the thick snow, and felt a sudden stabbing pain through her left heel as her foot slammed into the pavement. Curling around the pain, she tumbled out of the drift and rolled onto the pavement, the breath knocked from her body.

Shouting above her dragged her from her stunned state. When she looked up, Mrs. West was leaning out of the window, screaming.

"I'll catch you, child! I'll catch you!"

Sobbing with the pain in her heel, she rolled to her knees, then somehow found her feet, her body driven on by one aching truth: she couldn't let Mrs. West catch her. She could never go back.

She was running then, somehow, snow flaking from her clothes, the dreadful cold and the pain far less piercing than the fear that drove her on, and she ran straight up to the doors of the church with their beautiful beribboned wreath. She grasped at them, pulled back with all her might, but they were shut fast. That lovely place of light and music was closed to her.

"Holly Gray!" thundered Mrs. West.

A sob tore from her. Like a hunted animal, she turned and bolted from streetlight to streetlight, not knowing where she was going, only what she was running from. And run she would, she resolved, till she dropped, rather than go back.

* * * *

It had been difficult to keep Holly's gift away from the other boys, but with an effort, Theodore had managed it. He could feel the little lump of it against his chest where he had tucked it into his shirt, wrapped in some rags he'd torn from his workhouse shirt.

Mrs. West would probably cane him for it, but it would be worth it if he could only see a smile on poor Holly's face. If he could only tell her how sorry he was that he hadn't been the one to take the blame, and how grateful he was that she had kept quiet about him.

Perhaps the gift would help him say the words that he could not. He slipped out of the silent dormitory, the little gift held tight against his stomach, and scampered into the dark hallway.

Keeping one hand against the cold wall for a sense of direction, he crept forward, gently slipping the gift out from under his shirt. He couldn't wait to see Holly's face when he gave it to her, even if it was shrouded in shadow.

He came to a stop at their usual place, stood listening, waiting for a sound from her. She wasn't there. He heard no screams and no sobbing.

It seemed impossible. Surely Holly would be upset, after the night in the refractory ward? Surely she would slip from the dormitory and come looking for him? He would go looking for her if she needed to be guided. But he heard nothing.

He sat in the darkness waiting for a long, long time. There was no sound, and no one came. At times he dozed a little despite the bitter cold; occasionally he heard the distant sounds of the last few carollers singing the last few songs of this

Christmas night. Eventually, when he heard the church bell strike four, he knew he had no choice but to go back.

Slowly, his body stiff with the cold, Theodore laid the gift down on the cold stone for Holly to find by some miracle. It was everything he had: a bit of beef and baked potato from dinner, wrapped in rags; and a tiny doll, twisted together with straw, the eyes picked out with little pieces of coal, a charcoal mouth drawn in a wide, crude smile.

He stared down at the small, smiling doll for a long moment before lowering his head and slinking back to the dormitory. The world felt as though a jagged hole had been ripped in it. It was cold and empty without her. Maybe she would come tomorrow.

* * * *

It was the wind that was the worst part.

It knifed through Holly's workhouse dresses, laughing at the frayed linen as though it was nothing, until her flesh shrank and goose-pimpled from the cold. She wrapped her arms around herself in a bid to keep it away, but it did nothing except chill her arms all the more.

The wind ran its cold fingernails over her neck and belly, her back and thin little hips. There were times when it was so strong that it punched snow against her face with a force that made her stagger backwards, gasping with pain and surprise.

Her feet felt like leaden lumps attached to worthless legs that could barely keep them shuffling forwards.

Her heart had been thudding for the first while – an hour? Two hours? Three? – after she escaped the workhouse; now, it seemed to flutter in her, unable to muster any more strength.

Wind… she needed to get out of the wind. The workhouse was far behind her, and the sounds of pursuing footsteps had faded into the night. Even the streets were all but abandoned; her small footprints were alone in the snow that covered the street.

Her weary eyes caught upon an alleyway. Earlier, she had tried sheltering in one, only to be chased away by an irate housewife. Perhaps this time would be different. Everyone had to be asleep by now. Stumbling and shivering, she made her way into the alley, and even though the snow still blew down upon her from above, the fact that she was sheltered from the wind felt like utter bliss.

Sagging to the ground, she curled up, knees to her chest, and lowered her head onto her knees. Every bone in her ached. Her left heel sent sharp pangs up her leg.

Delicious sleep was reaching for her when she heard it: harsh, heavy breathing, somewhere to her right. A quiver of dreadful terror shot down her spine. She looked up, and in the light of the nearby streetlamp, an awful visage glowered at her: sallow skin, sunken cheeks, yellowed eyes that rolled madly in their sockets, draped with greasy hair.

"What… are you doing… here… little girl?" hissed a voice that seemed to rise up from the pit of London's foulest sewer.

A scream tore from Holly's throat. Cackling, the old tramp snatched at her.

She ducked his yellowing claws with inches to spare and bolted into the street again, her heart rattling wildly in her chest.

She ran until her tired limbs found a corner between two houses, which offered shelter from the wind even though it was carpeted in snow. Shaking and crying, she fell to her knees there, then to her side, hugging herself as she sobbed with fear.

A dog barked inside one of the houses. Holly froze, cowering against the snow, but it was too late. Gas lights clicked on. A window was thrown wide, and a strident voice thundered from within it.

"Oi! Get away from here, you urchin!" A stone flew through the air, landing in the snow beside Holly with a thud. "Get out of here!"

Holly sat up, staring at the window and the silhouetted figure beyond with rising disbelief. Why was she not allowed to exist quietly in this corner? Had her life become a crime?

Another stone slammed into the ground beside her. Either way, she had no choice. Too tired to run this time, she dragged herself to her feet and stumbled away down the icy street, her feet slipping on the cobblestones.

If she couldn't sleep somewhere out of the cold, she would have to walk if she wanted to keep warm until the sun came up. Arms around herself, she lowered her head and stumbled on.

* * * *

Even fear could not drive Holly on forever. There was only the vaguest suggestion of dawn in the distant eastern sky, and only the faintest stirring of traffic on the street, when her legs would bear her no longer.

Vaguely, she saw that the buildings around her were small, squat homes, rows of tiny and flaking doors all crowded close together, cottages built right onto the street. She stumbled up to the nearest one, her eyes barely grazing the number thirteen that was painted and peeling on the door.

There was little in the way of a nook there, but perhaps she could turn her face, at least, out of the wind. It was the only doorway in the street that had a wreath hanging from it; a poor little wreath, only mistletoe and a few spruce twigs, with a single yellow ribbon damp and sagging on the bottom.

Perhaps the wreath meant that whoever lived here had a tiny bit of that goldenness she had seen in the church – that Christmas candlelight – in their soul. Enough not to deny a small girl a place to rest for a few minutes.

She collapsed in the doorway, legs sprawled onto the pavement, and shielded her face with one arm, her cheek against the coarse wood of the door. The cold sucked at her limbs. Her hands and feet burned. Her shivers had stopped. The cold became numbness, and just as the numbness began to turn into warmth, a deep dark sleep dragged Holly into its deathly embrace.

* * * *

The door swung open, and Holly fell full-length onto a stone floor.

A yelp of terror ripped from her mouth as she fell, sprawling, jolts of pain shooting through her half-frozen joints. She scrabbled for a second, her eyes burning in the brightness of what must have been morning sunshine. Summer sunshine, perhaps. Even though she could barely feel her toes and fingers, she felt a sudden rush of warmth running through her body, intolerable warmth.

Boots. She was looking at hobnailed boots standing on the stone floor in front of her. They looked like they would be painful if they kicked.

"Now, then." The voice was a harsh, croaking sound. "What have we here?"

Holly sat up, clutching at her dress, amazed to find it soaked with snow instead of sweat. Her fingertips were blue; goosebumps trembled on her arms, yet she felt she was burning.

"Well, then?" barked the voice. "Can you speak, child?"

Holly looked up into a face as wizened as a roasted chestnut, two small bright eyes like raisins in the centre. The mouth was puckered as the little old woman, her hair a wild white shock around her face like a halo of mist, peered at Holly.

"I can speak," Holly whispered. She tried to get to her feet, but her legs wouldn't let her, and she sagged to the ground. "I'm sorry."

"Now what are you sorry for?" The old woman stepped over Holly and slammed the door.

Darkness filled the room – a tiny, cottage kitchen – for a heart-stopping instant before Holly's eyes adjusted to the cold slant of sunlight coming in through the window.

"I... don't know," Holly whispered. She was shivering, but she tugged at her dress, wanting to peel one of them off.

The woman's little hard hand shot out and slapped hers away with a force that made her squeal. "What are you doing, child?"

"I'm so hot," said Holly.

"No, you're not. You're frozen half to death." The little raisin eyes widened. "I've heard tell people do such things when they've frozen. Come here!"

She grabbed Holly by the arm and dragged her over to a small coal fire that glowed in the hearth. Adding a few more bricks of coal, the woman seized a rug from the little bed nearby and threw it around Holly's shoulders.

"What... what are you doing?" Holly whimpered.

"Drink." The woman thrust a mug of tea into Holly's hands. It made her gasp with heat, but she did as she was told, because the woman's hard black eyes wouldn't let her disobey.

The heat left her bones slowly, replaced by a bitter cold that chattered her teeth. The woman put another rug around her and sat slowly in a creaky chair by the fireplace.

"Workhouse child?" she grunted.

Holly lowered her head. "Y-y-yes," she stammered, her jaw jumping helplessly from the cold.

The woman grunted again. "Dreadful places. I grew up in one." She tossed another coal onto the fire. "You'll have to earn your keep, understand?"

"My keep?" Holly whispered.

"I'm a washerwoman. It's hard work. I need a girl to help me." The woman's eyes narrowed. "Or did you want to go back onto the streets?"

Holly drew nearer to the fire. "Please... no."

"Alright then. You can stay here. What do they call you?"

"Holly Gray."

"I'm Margaret Stout." The woman folded her arms. "You shall call me Peggy."

Holly sat still, staring at her.

"Don't stare so, child. Drink your tea," barked Peggy.

Holly drank her tea and started into the glowing coals, and somehow Christmas was in this tiny cottage as it had been in the shining church.

Part Two

Chapter Five

Four Years Later

The first snow of the winter was falling. Next month it would be Christmas, and the thought sent a wonderful pang of excitement through Holly's belly.

She strode across the market square with firm, steady strides, dragging a little handcart piled high with dirty laundry. There was a little basket crooked over her elbow, and she gazed around, delighted by the fat white flakes that filtered through the air. Just this morning Mrs. Clarksworth had been saying how she thought it might snow early this year, and she was right. Only late November, and the snowflakes came down thickly, kissing Holly's skin where they landed on her bare cheeks.

A few moments later, Holly turned off the street and into the little market square, and a scene of glorious wonder greeted her. The snow was still thin, but there was enough of it to pepper every roof and cobblestone, and it was coming down faster now, turning the familiar old square into a wonderland of falling flakes.

A snatch of music caught her ear. There was a young man with a fiddle on the street corner, and this afternoon he was playing "Greensleeves". Holly couldn't wait for him to start playing her favourite carols in a few weeks' time. Immediately, "Joy to the World" leaped into her heart, its words echoing in her mind. *Joy to the world, the Lord is come. Let Earth receive her King!*

She hummed along with the music in her mind as she hurried up to the nearest stall, her cart bump-bumping along behind her. In her free hand, she clutched tightly the little pouch of money that Peggy's clients had given her, grateful to have their clothes delivered even in the snow.

The stall was manned by a jolly young fellow with roses in his cheeks and a thick head of ginger curls. "Evenin', Holly!" he said. "How can I help you?"

"Please may I have a loaf of bread?" Holly phrased the question carefully, just as Peggy had taught her.

Her elegant words made the young baker grin. "Here you are, luv." He placed a stout loaf of fresh, steaming white bread on the table.

"Thank you, sir." Holly smiled back at him, taking the bread and going on her way.

She wandered around the square, buying a few more small things – a string of gristly grey sausages from the butcher, a bit of cheese from the dairyman, some carrots and a turnip from the grocer.

Carefully, she packed these into her shopping basket and set the basket in the handcart, then turned her steps through the snowy streets towards home. Even though the snow was cold against her skin, she didn't mind. Soon there would be wreaths on all of these doorways, and the very thought made it seem as though the air itself was thick with magic.

Holly pulled her scarf up to her chin and adjusted her hat over her ears. The hat was much too big, had a few holes in it, and was missing the pom-pom on top, but it kept her ears warm well enough even if wisps of her hair straggled loose from it and blew in the wind.

She tried not to think about that other Christmas – a little less than four years ago now. That time was far behind her. Life was filled with light and hope now, and she had learned that though the church full of candlelight had been locked that Christmas day, there was plenty of light to be found even in modest places in this city.

Her footsteps took her to the row of little cottages where her life had changed on that fateful day. Reaching the familiar doorway of number thirteen, she pushed it open, dragging the little handcart inside.

"Peggy, I'm home!" she called.

"Back here!" croaked the hoarse old voice of Peggy Stout.

Holly placed the shopping basket on the table and towed the handcart into the back room, which was filled with steam. Peggy was bent over a large vat of hot water, poking at a pile of clothes inside with a long stick. Soap suds bubbled against the lip of the vat. The one beside her was equally hot, containing clear water, and multiple lines of strings hung up across the rest of the room held piece after piece of drying laundry.

"The Clarksworths sent their regards and gave us tuppence extra," said Holly. She grasped another stick and began to lift clean clothes from the soapy water into the rinse water.

"And the Nolan's?" asked Peggy.

"This is mostly theirs." Holly gestured to the handcart. "And they want it all done in the next two days for a party."

"Of course they do." Peggy rolled her eyes. "Best get cracking with it tonight, then. Otherwise it won't dry in time."

Holly's aching legs and empty belly cried out in protest, but she ignored them both and continued her work. They worked quickly, efficiently, and in silence. Peggy piled the dirty clothes into the soapy water, mixed them around and drubbed them on a scrubbing board; Holly rinsed them and hung them up. Her back soon ached, and even her hard hands grew tired and shrivelled after only a few minutes.

At last, the Nolan's' laundry was hanging up to dry, every piece more expensive than all of Peggy and Holly's clothes put together. They emptied the filthy water from the vats, and only then retired to the cottage kitchen for supper.

Peggy's eyes brightened when Holly produced the fresh white loaf. "Still good and warm," she grunted, slicing thick chunks of bread and cheese for supper. The vegetables and sausages would be for the next several days. Holly knew that she should enjoy the bread while it was fresh; it would have to last for the better part of a week.

"Will we still be able to have something nice for Christmas Eve?" Holly asked timidly.

"Why, that's weeks away, child," Peggy grumbled.

"I know." Holly hung her head. "I just—I'm excited for Christmas."

Peggy gave her one of her rare smiles. "Of course we'll have something nice. Sit down, child. Perhaps it won't be roast goose – but maybe a roast chicken, and some potatoes. Perhaps even a bit of fruit cake to share."

Excitement bubbled in Holly's heart as she took her place at the table. "I saw the young man with the fiddle in the square," she said, tearing off a piece of bread after Peggy had mumbled grace. "I hope he plays carols again, closer to Christmastime."

"Oh, so do I. Carols are my favourite part of Christmas." Peggy's face softened, as it only ever did when she talked about Christmas. "My sister and I used to sing 'Hark the Herald Angels Sing' all the time before she married that farmer and moved to the country."

Holly often wondered why Peggy hadn't moved with her sister, instead choosing to stay here in this cottage and plod through the drudgery of a washerwoman's life. She decided not to ask, though. Whenever she did, Peggy would only snort that she didn't need anyone else's charity.

"I sang Christmas carols with a friend sometimes in the workhouse," she said.

"Oh?" Peggy raised an eyebrow. "Was the friend this Theodore that you've told me about?"

"Yes." Holly bit into her bread, enjoying its fluffy freshness. "He was the only friend I ever had, before you."

"I'm no friend of yours. You work for me," grumbled Peggy, but she picked up the pitcher of milk and added a little more to Holly's cup even though there wasn't much left.

Holly smiled at her, but Peggy pretended not to notice. "We used to sing very softly, just the words of the carols we'd heard at the church next door." She lowered her head. "Theodore was the only person I knew who cared about Christmas back then."

"Christmas is about hope, forgiveness, joy, and love," said Peggy. "People who don't have any of that in their hearts – well, sometimes they hate it."

"Theodore had all of those things." Holly stared out of the window. "I miss him. Especially at Christmas."

Peggy reached over the table with a gnarled little old hand and patted Holly's fingers. "Well, you won't have much time to miss him tomorrow. We've got to finish ironing the Nolan's' clothes."

Holly nodded and turned back to her bread and cheese. In her mind, she could still hear "Joy to the World", the familiar words threading through her consciousness of their own accord.

Let every heart prepare him room, and heaven and nature sing!

* * * *

The bigger boy was clothed in the same ugly workhouse stripes as everyone else, and his fist slammed into the little boy's chest with a force that sent the child stumbling backwards and crashing to the ground with a yelp of pain.

"I told you to move over!" the big boy thundered.

None of the servers paid any mind to the scene taking place at the table by the fire. The littler boy, whose clothes were still new and unfaded, began to cry – big, broken sobs that sounded worn-in and practiced, like he had been crying very often lately. It was seldom that one heard a boy his age – he must have been eight or so – cry in the workhouse dormitory. Most of the boys had learned to give up on sorrow at his age, and to choose violence instead.

The big boy chuckled and grabbed the littler boy's plate. "Your sausages are mine now – every night, understand?"

A small hand tugged at Theodore's sleeve. "Theo, you've got to do something."

Theo had just sat down to his own meal after helping the tiniest boys to gather theirs, and he felt a wave of exhaustion wash through him as he looked up and saw the scene unfold. He had spent the entire day shielding the flock of little ones that followed him everywhere from the other bullies, and he'd been looking forward to eating his sausages warm.

"Here." He pushed the plate towards the little ones at his table. "Keep it safe until I get back, would you?"

"Yes, Theo," whispered their ringleader, a boy named Nigel Hawthorne whose words whistled between the gap in his front teeth.

Theodore got up and strode across the dining hall to the table by the fire. The smaller boy, the new one, was still sobbing on the ground while the bigger boy snatched up sausages from his plate and sucked them down with his fingers. Theodore knew him well. He was one of the pettier bullies, an improbably broad-shouldered boy named Thomas Green.

"Thomas, that's not yours." Theodore kept his voice slow and reasonable.

Reason had never worked on boys like him. Thomas glared at him out of small, desperate, piggy eyes. "Stay out of this."

Theodore crouched down and helped the small boy to his feet, dusting off his clothes. "Give him back his supper. You know that you've had more than enough already."

"It's never enough," Thomas hissed, clutching the plate close to his body.

The other boys' attention was riveted on Theodore and Thomas. Theo didn't want this to come down to a fight. The other boys would begin chanting, and then Mrs. West would get involved – something no one wanted. Thomas' eyes darted towards the servers' table, as though he, too, were considering this.

Then, Thomas' grip tightened on the plate. "If he wants it, let him come and take it."

This inspired a renewed bout of sobbing from the new boy. Theodore stepped forward, placing his body between the new boy and Thomas, and folded his arms. Thomas swallowed visibly. He had to tip back his head to look Theodore in the eye.

"Give it back," Theo said quietly.

Thomas glanced around, but if he had any cronies, they had abandoned him. Slowly, reluctantly, he held out the plate.

"Thank you," said Theo courteously. He grasped the new boy's arm. "Come along, now. You're going to sit with me from now on."

Bubbling profuse thanks through a veil of tears, the new boy trailed after Theodore back to the table. The other small boys regarded him in silence. Theodore noticed, sighing quietly to himself, that most of his food had disappeared down their hungry little gullets already. They had left him one sausage and a piece of coarse brown bread.

"What's your name?" Theodore asked, settling the new boy beside him.

The little boy took several gulping bites of his meal before answering. "Steele. Harry Steele."

"Well, you're going to be all right, Harry," said Theodore. "These boys are all your friends, and you'll be safe."

"Theo takes care of us," lisped Nigel. He put a skinny arm around Harry's shoulders. "You'll be all right."

"Thank you," Harry whimpered. "Thank you."

Theodore ruffled his hair and finished his own meal, keeping a watchful eye in case any bullies thought they could interrupt his little boys' meal. Once they had all finished, he marshalled them into a line and marched them up to the front of the dining hall to lay down all of their plates.

Nigel's skinny little hand slipped into Theo's. "Will you tell us a story tonight, Theo?" he whispered. "The one about the rabbit?"

Theodore smiled. "You've asked for the rabbit story every night all week, Nigel, and it's still weeks before Christmas."

"What's it about?" asked Harry, his fear soothed into curiosity.

"It's about a little rabbit who leads the fox away from her friends, to keep them safe," said Nigel. "Right on Christmas Eve. A very brave rabbit."

Theodore smiled sadly. In his story, the rabbit found her way back to her family every single time. He could still see Holly's big, bright eyes, still feel her small hand in his own. If only he could find her again...

"Theodore Bunton!"

A chill ran down Theo's spine. He stopped, looking up. Mrs. West had stepped into the dining hall, and she was holding a slip of notepaper with his name scribbled on it. He wasn't surprised she couldn't remember it. He seldom gave her reason to notice him.

"Theo..." Nigel's hand tightened on his, terrified.

"It's all right, Nigel." Theodore squeezed the small hand gently. "It's all right."

"Theodore Bunton!" yelled Mrs. West.

Theodore took a deep breath and squared his shoulders. "Yes, Mrs. West?"

The matron's sharp, unyielding eyes found him and rested there. He felt a terrible bolt of cold lance through his belly.

"Come with me," she ordered.

Theodore looked down at Nigel, who was clinging to his hand so tightly that his fingers had gone almost completely white.

"I beg your pardon, ma'am," he said, summoning all the politeness he had, "where are we going?"

Mrs. West's eyes bored through him. "Don't make a scene, child," she spat. "You know you are fourteen. I've already been gracious to you, but you're far too big to stay here any longer. You're joining the men."

Theodore felt as though every cell in his body had been turned into ice. He froze completely, ignoring Nigel's soft snivelling and the piping questions from the other little boys.

He had not known he was to join the men. He had no idea how old he was. Nobody really did. Just like the name he'd been given when he was taken into the orphanage, his age, was whatever they entered into the orphanage records. The workhouse had been his home ever since he could remember.

Mrs. West's face was getting angrier and angrier. It was several moments, and she had almost reached him, when Theodore's ears cleared of buzzing and he realized that she was demanding he come with her. The little boys were clutching at his pants, at his fingers, crying, about to scream.

"Stop that fuss!" Mrs. West roared. "Stop it!"

"Mrs. West, if you please." Theodore summoned all of his strength to turn and face her. "They will let me go quietly if you give me a few minutes with them. Please, ma'am, I beg of you."

Mrs. West glanced at the boys, then at Theodore, and her lips loosened from their usual thin line. "One minute, Bunton. That's all the time you have."

"Thank you, ma'am," Theodore choked out. He crouched down by the boys, gripped Nigel by the shoulders, and squeezed him tightly. "I'm going away now."

A chorus of dismay rose up from them.

"Hush!" Theodore said, sharply but not harshly.

The boys all fell silent.

"I'm going away, and there's nothing I can do about it, but you are all strong enough to be here without me." Theodore squeezed Nigel's shoulders. "You are in charge now, Nigel, do you understand? You must help the little boys. Do you understand?"

Tears coursing down his cheeks, Nigel nodded.

"Be strong now," said Theodore. "Take them to the dormitory. Help them to wash their hands and faces." He straightened. "Go."

Nigel took a breath that swelled his shoulders. He reached for the hands of two other small boys and they strode out of the dining hall in a sniffling line.

"Are you ready *now*?" snarled Mrs. West.

Theodore straightened. "Yes, ma'am."

She beckoned. "Come."

He followed her out of the dining hall, keeping his back as straight as he could until he was sure the little boys couldn't see him. But when they walked into the hallway, everything within him broke, and he trailed after Mrs. West with tears rushing down his cheeks like blood.

* * * *

This was Holly's favourite task in the washerwoman world. Peggy's old knees made it difficult for her to make the trip on a day such as this one, when snow lay deep on all of the paths and treacherous patches of ice lurked everywhere, so she was walking alone on this day; but despite the many inches of snow that had fallen overnight, the sun was balmy, and beauty surrounded her.

This part of London was only an hour's walk from Peggy's cottage, yet it might as well have existed in a different world. The handcart crunched after her, and though it was heavy going in the snow, Holly still had time to gaze at the tall and beautiful houses that towered up on either side of the broad street.

They were always lovely, with their high windows and jutting turrets and pillared corners, but she knew that soon they would be lovelier than ever now.

It was the first day of December, and soon people would begin to hang their decorations. Wreaths and bunting would hang wherever Holly looked.

There would be vibrant sprigs of bright red holly decorating every post and doorway, and most of the homes would have a snow-dusted spruce tree wrapped in shimmering tinsel in the garden.

Even better would be the beauty she would see through the massive windows: trees decked out in sweets and baubles, with huge parcels tied up in satin bows stacked deep at their feet.

Even though there were no decorations up yet, the park looked lovely today. It was carpeted thickly in glittering snow, with flakes settling on all of its gates and lampposts. The hedges were bright with berries. Her step quickened with eagerness as she reached the gate.

When she looked over the gate, she spotted Caroline Mills at once. The girl was sitting at a bench nearby, reading, wrapped up in her thick fur coat despite the balmy sunshine.

"Hello, Caroline!" Holly called out.

The girl rose to her feet, her expensive satin dress rustling. Her eyes brightened, and she lowered the brand new hardcover. "Holly! Come and sit by me for a moment."

"Won't your governess mind?" Holly asked.

Caroline tossed her head. "She doesn't mind anything as long as she isn't in trouble with Papa, and what Papa doesn't know can't hurt him."

Grinning, Holly opened the gate and headed into the park, remembering how the unlikely friendship between an upper-middle-class businessman's daughter and this washerwoman's assistant had begun.

* * * *

It was almost Christmas two years ago. The park's lampposts were all wrapped in ribbons, with a beautiful big wreath on the gate. Holly's feet stung from a long day of walking, and she had a heavy load of laundry in the cart behind her when she paused by the gate for a little breather. It was then that she heard the voice.

"Curse you, you stupid dress! Curse you!"

Holly could almost instantly forgive the vulgarity in the voice thanks to the sheer exasperation that it held. She looked left and right, and her eyes alit upon a colourful figure standing by the hedge off to her left, amid a collection of snow-dusted rose bushes.

It was a young girl, close to Holly's age, but wearing a beautifully embroidered silk dress and a coat trimmed elegantly with white mink. The girl was twisting this way and that, struggling to grasp the back of her dress, which was nastily tangled in the thorns of one of the rosebushes.

"Curse you!" cried the girl, tugging hard.

"Miss. Miss!" Holly left the handcart and let herself into the park. "Wait! You'll tear it. Let me help you."

The girl stopped and looked at Holly. Her cheeks were flushed with exertion, but this could not hide the smooth whiteness of her skin. She wore her blonde hair in curls around her face, and her eyes were strikingly blue, her most prominent feature; Holly noticed these long before she realized that the girl had a rather recessive chin and very round cheeks.

"Oh, would you be so good?" the girl panted. "It's hopelessly knotted, and I can't see behind my back."

Holly was surprised that this well-dressed girl would address her so civilly, considering that her dress was ragged and much-mended, and that she wore shoes two sizes too big.

"Of course, miss," she said. "Hold still, and I'll untangle it for you in a jiffy."

"Thank you."

The girl stood, fidgeting, while Holly gently pried the beautiful fabric away from the rose thorns that had so cruelly ensnared it. It was some of the nicest fabric she had ever had the pleasure of touching; there were layers of silk and tulle that rustled wonderfully while she worked with it. Pricking her fingers a few times, she tugged the rosebushes away, and the dress fell free.

"Oh! Thank you." The girl turned to her, smoothing down the back of her dress.

She seemed in no hurry to leave, so Holly asked, "How did it get so tangled?"

"Oh, I was hiding from my governess," said the girl flippantly.

"Hiding? Why?" Holly's eyes widened. "Is she cruel?"

"Cruel! No. Just stupid, I suppose – or at the very least, very annoying." The girl grinned mischievously. "I think she's still looking for me down by the spruce grove over there. I told her we were playing hide and seek."

"Oh." Holly couldn't help giggling at the mischievousness in the girl's voice.

"Thank you for helping me. I'm sure Mama would not have been amused if I had torn my dress." The girl gripped her rustling skirt and made a very pretty little curtsy. "My name is Caroline Mills. What's yours?"

Holly curtsied back, clumsily. She had never curtsied or been curtsied to before. "Holly Gray."

"Holly! That's a pretty name, don't you think?"

"It is." Holly smiled shyly. "I was born on Christmas Day."

"That's wonderful! Well, it must be almost your birthday, then." Caroline giggled. "What fun!"

"Caroline!"

The furious voice came, predictably, from the spruce grove, from whence a pudgy and ineffectual woman in a little hat that was threatening to fly away came trudging up the hill.

"Caroline, you bad girl! Come back here at once!" she cried.

Caroline grimaced. "I'd best be going, then. It was nice meeting you, Holly." She smiled. "Maybe we'll see each other again. My family has just moved here, and I have no one to talk to."

"I pass here often." Holly glanced at the governess, backing away, knowing full well that the woman would not be amused by Caroline speaking with a ragamuffin like her. Still, she hardly ever met with anyone her age, so she allowed herself to stay long enough to give Caroline a wide smile. "I hope I'll see you again."

"Me too, Miss Holly Gray." Caroline beamed at her. "Goodbye!"

She hurried to meet her governess, and Holly hurried to meet her handcart with a fresh little bounce in her step.

* * * *

Caroline had become Holly's first friend close to her age, since Theo, and now Holly sat down on the bench beside the other girl. The governess, ever furious about their friendship, pouted over her book on another bench nearby.

"We'll have to go back soon, Caroline," she called. "The weather's going to turn, I can feel it."

"What nonsense!" Caroline gave a bubbling laugh. "Anyway, how are you, dear Holly?"

"I'm very well. We're busy at this time of year—there are plenty of parties and gatherings, and I think there will only be more as we come nearer to Christmas," said Holly. "What about you?"

"Oh, I'm also busy. There are so frightfully many parties, like you said, and they can be so boring." Caroline giggled. "Papa says in a few years' time I'll have to find suitors at these parties, but honestly that sounds even more boring to me."

The girls giggled together, and Holly's heart was filled with joy. Caroline might not be Theo, but she was still grateful for the gift of her friendship, even if she only saw her for a few minutes at a time on her way to laundry deliveries.

* * * *

Despite the cold that nipped at Holly's nose and fingers, and the exhaustion that weighed down her limbs, she found that she had a bright little skip in her step as she reached the narrow street where she lived. The handcart was weighed down with dirty laundry, but the Nolan's had been given their clothes, and she knew that a hot supper would be waiting for her just through the door to number thirteen. She pushed it open, stepping into the little cottage.

"I'm home, Peggy!" she called out.

There was no response from the laundry room. Puzzled, Holly dragged the cart towards it. Peggy hadn't mentioned that she was going out.

"Here, child."

The voice was a tiny croak from Holly's right, and it made her jump. She looked up and saw Peggy sitting hunched over by the fire, a blanket drawn tight around her bony old shoulders. Her hands clutched a mug of steaming tea, and they were shaking.

Fear jolted through Holly's belly, as a cold lance through her. She had never seen Peggy sitting down with a mug of tea during the day before, except at lunchtime, and it was now four or five in the afternoon. A glance towards the laundry room told her that the day's laundry was still lying in a dirty pile on the ground.

Something was horribly wrong.

She was trembling as she stepped forward. "Peggy? Wh- what's the matter?"

"Don't fuss so, child." Peggy's voice was a raw, harsh croak. "I'm all right."

Holly left the handcart standing right in the kitchen where she'd left it and hurried over to Peggy. She took off her holey gloves and pressed the back of her hand to the old woman's forehead. Peggy pulled away with a hiss of annoyance, but not before Holly could feel the dreadful, sizzling heat against her skin.

"You're very hot, Peggy," said Holly tearfully.

"It's just a cold, child," barked Peggy, but the words were swallowed up in a series of rough, raw coughs that seemed to be tearing apart her chest from the inside out. Her body trembled uncontrollably. She doubled up in front of the fire, tea slopping from her mug and spilling onto the ground.

"Peggy..." Holly whispered.

"The laundry," Peggy croaked. "The laundry must be done." She put down the half-empty mug, ignoring the spilled tea on the floor, and lunged to her feet. At once, with a cry of pain and weakness, she raised a hand to her face and sank back onto the stool.

Holly grasped her arm, stopping her from falling, and settled the old woman back upon her stool. She wrapped the blanket around her shoulders once more and returned the tea to her hands. "I'll do the laundry later tonight, Peggy."

"It needs doing," Peggy croaked.

"Of course it does. But first I'm going to buy you medicine." Holly swallowed the lump of terror in her throat. "I'm going to buy you some medicine and it's going to make you better."

Peggy looked up, a sharp retort already upon her lips, but she swallowed it at whatever it was that she saw in Holly's eyes.

She sagged, seeming to shrink several inches, and took a shaky sip of the tea.

"All right," she croaked.

Her assent in itself was cause for Holly to be terrified. Reaching for the mantelpiece, she took a few pennies from Peggy's life savings – which amounted to half-a-crown – from the cup where she kept the money. "I'll be back soon," Holly promised, and hastened out into the cold day.

Clouds had blown over, veiling the sun. London seemed to have lost much of its colour. Even the red of the holly berries she saw on the bushes in some of the gardens seemed to have faded.

Suddenly, the thought of the coming Christmas seemed far less bright.

Chapter Six.

Theodore's hands were already blistered and bleeding, and it was not yet noon.

His back ached appallingly from the way he was sitting on the ground, his legs splayed in front of him, a large piece of stone lying between his knees.

Blood smeared the handle of the hammer he gripped in his right hand, a chisel tightly clenched in his left.

Despite the bitter cold that howled around his ears and chapped the red and bruised skin on the backs of his hands, his palms were sweating, and sweat ran into his blisters till they burned.

Ignoring the burn, he raised the hammer and drove it into the chisel, again and again, cracks spreading out across the piece of stone. Small bits began to break off, and Theodore gritted his teeth against the pain, hammering again. And again.

It did not matter to the supervisor that his hands were still tender with childhood, that he had only been here on the men's side for two weeks.

It did not matter that Theodore had never done such physical work before or that he could feel the flesh melting from his bones already or that his hands were rough and bleeding from his merciless work. All that mattered was that Theodore had to produce a set amount of crushed stone every day, and if he did not, then Heaven help him.

Theodore had never been to the refractory ward, but he had seen the faces of the boys who had, and they appalled him.

The stone shattered at last into hundreds of small pieces, and Theodore gathered them up carefully, thrusting them into a pile. He reached for another piece of large stone and a voice floated across the stone yard towards him.

"Give it me!" it hissed.

Theodore glanced sideways as he braced the next stone between his knees. He sat in the back corner of the stone yard, where the draft from the gate blew directly upon him. It was where all the other younger men – boys, really, fourteen years and older – were sitting; the bigger men all sat in the other, sheltered corners of the yard.

"I told you to give me that stone!" growled the voice again.

It was a scraggly young man of eighteen or so who sat ahead and to the left of Theodore. He had thin arms and wild eyes, and he was holding out a bony claw of a hand to one of the other youngest boys in the stone yard.

Paul had been a broad-shouldered, swaggering youth when Mrs. West had taken him out of Theodore's dormitory a few months before. Now, he was pale and thin and unrecognizable, huddled over a pitiful mound of crushed stone.

"No," he whispered, pulling his pile of stone away from the young man.

"I don't want to be whipped. Give it to me," growled the young man.

Paul's wild eyes darted from the young man to the supervisor and back, but no help was forthcoming. The boy's shoulders trembled. Theodore had defended many a little boy from Paul, but now he was a little boy himself, and Theodore could see that he was afraid.

Glancing at the supervisor, Theodore saw that the man was standing in a far corner in a scrap of sunlight, smoking and ignoring his charges. He often did – until the time came to examine each man's work for the day.

"This is your last chance, guttersnipe," spat the young man, curling his hand into an ugly fist.

Theodore rose. "Leave him alone."

There was a beat of total silence. Theodore's quiet voice seemed to ring in this corner of the stone yard; every man nearby froze in his work, their heads all turning to stare at him.

The young man's fist tightened. "What was that?"

"I told you to leave him alone." Theodore bunched his own hands into fists, painfully aware that he was the youngest boy here. "Break your own stone. Don't take his."

The young man rose to his feet slowly, as though pulled upwards by puppet strings. He took two deliberate steps towards Theodore. "Or what?" he growled. "Are you going to try to stop me?"

Theodore spread his hands. "No one wants to fight. But it's not right for you to take Paul's stone."

The young man's face twisted in an ugly sneer. Paul sat very still, his face ashen, eyes flickering from Theodore to his opponent and back again.

The young man spat. "Well, are you going to stop me?"

Theodore raised his chin, a terrible dread curdling in his belly. "If I have to."

The young man snickered and struck towards him, and the blow missed Theodore by a hair's breadth. He stumbled sideways, hands held out. The next blow landed squarely on Theodore's jaw with a force that snapped darkness down over his eyes. He landed heavily on his back among the crushed bits of stone, and as the other men roared and his enemy straddled him and began to rain punch after punch down upon Theodore's head, all that he could do was to throw his arms up over his face and pray for it to end.

* * * *

Holly bent over the steaming heat of the rinse tub, her chest heaving with effort, her arms trembling uncontrollably as she gripped the corners of the huge fitted sheet.

The bed that this sheet was made for must be enormous, she thought, sucking in heavy breaths as she clung to the sheet. Five or six times the size of Peggy's cot in the corner of the cottage. Who needed a bed that size?

The sheet was proportionately huge, and thick for the winter, and waterlogged.

Normally, it was a hard task for two of them together to haul the sheet out of this tub. Now, Peggy lay on her cot, sleeping feverishly, her cheeks very flushed, her gnarled hands twitching on the covers. Holly was all alone.

"Come on," she moaned. "Come on!"

With a gargantuan effort, she leaned back, hauling the sheet halfway out of the water. Panting and struggling, she strove to pull it all the way out of the tub. Almost there—she had to be careful not to let go, or it would slip back down again. Almost—

Peggy sat up with a long gasp. Holly froze, staring at her. Clutching a hand to her chest, the old woman began to cough, great and dreadful coughs that seemed to swallow her entire being. Her breaths came in harsh crackles, each more laboured than the last.

"Peggy!" Holly gasped. She let go of the sheet, ignoring the heavy *plop* as it landed back in the water, and rushed to Peggy's side. Grasping the glass bottle by the bed, she poured some of its contents into a spoon.

Peggy shook her head, still coughing uncontrollably, and held out a hand.

"You must, Peggy, you must." Holly guided the spoon into Peggy's mouth. The old lady swallowed with difficulty and sagged back against her pillow, exhausted, her eyes very red. They fluttered closed, and the fever dream claimed her again.

Holly's arms felt utterly wrung out from laundry, and that sheet was still there, waiting in the tub.

She lowered her head, resting it on the edge of Peggy's straw mattress, trembling with exhaustion. She had been doing this for a full week now.

She wasn't sure how much longer she could go on alone.

* * * *

Theodore chose the seat that no one wanted. It was at the front of the dining hall, right under the eyes of the supervisor, and a harsh draft rushed in from beneath the door. The bitterly cold air swirled around Theodore's ankles, making him shiver as he clutched his bowl of thin beef stew and hard bread.

When he had been a very little boy, he had felt just as he felt now. Alone, exposed, afraid, and starving. The other boys had knocked his bowl from his hands, thrown him to the ground, called him names that stung his soul.

When he had become one of the bigger boys, he had been determined that none of the little ones should ever feel the way he had felt then.

Yet now he was the little one again. Now his eyes kept darting to where the bigger men were sitting, grumbling over their dinner. With any luck, he could choke down his stew before the men paid any attention to him.

It was a little different in the dining hall, at least. Unlike the young boys, the men were dangerous, and the supervisor seldom allowed an all-out riot to take place here. It was the stone yards that were the most dangerous.

Theodore's bruised body told him as much. He paused in eating, running a hand over his painful jaw, which stung with every bite.

The young man who had landed that blow on his jaw yesterday glanced his way, and Theodore quickly turned his attention back to his bowl, his heart pounding. Was there going to be another fight?

The dining hall door creaked, and as one, every man in the hall looked up. The loud sound of Mrs. West's boots upon the stone floor echoed around the hall as the matron marched into the room. She glanced over the assembled group, then down at a slip of paper in her hand.

"Bunton," she called out. "Theodore Bunton."

Theodore rose slowly to his feet, trembling. What had he done wrong this time?

Mrs. West's eyes raked over him. "Come with me," she said, turning and marching out of the dining hall.

The last time she had led him out of this room, it had brought disaster upon him. Theodore trembled, but he knew he had no choice but to follow her.

They walked down a hallway and into her office, which had a window overlooking the street. Outside, Theo noticed ice hanging in needle like spikes from eaves, and the ground covered in a grey sludge.

Mrs. West sat down behind her desk. Theodore had only been here once before: the day that he first came to the workhouse. He had had only a vague impression of this room then.

Mrs. West scribbled in a book. "Mr. Bunton, you are leaving."

Theodore's heart thudded. "Leaving?" He looked again at the street, and suddenly the snow seemed more deadly than beautiful.

"Yes," said Mrs. West. "You are joining a middle-class family, the Clifford's, as assistant gardener. Their head gardener is waiting for you down the hall." She gave him a sharp look. "I expect you to do the name of this workhouse proud, do you understand?"

"M-ma'am?" Theodore trembled, but now it was with hope. He was being given a job. He was going somewhere better! When he was a boy, a few of his friends had left – sold as stable lads or farm workers. Everyone had always envied them.

And now it was Theodore's turn.

Mrs. West frowned at him. "Go and change your clothes in the intake room, then," she barked. "Before I choose someone else." A small tear gleamed in her eye. "Go on lad," she said softly.

"Yes, ma'am. Thank you, ma'am," Theodore stuttered.

Mrs. West shook her head and looked down at her ledger again, and Theodore made his way down the hall on numb legs. He paused just outside the intake room, where a sour-faced man waited, a set of clothes over his arm. Theodore guessed that this must be the gardener for whom he would be working.

"I'm Theodore Bunton, sir." Theodore nodded to the man.

The gardener grunted and held out the clothes. "Get dressed."

It felt glorious to go into the intake room and strip off the ugly, striped clothes of the workhouse. The clothes that the gardener had given him were rough and simple, but they had no holes in them. In fact, Theodore thought as he pulled on a thick jacket, they might even be new.

The gardener grunted again as Theodore stepped out of the room. "Come. Let's go."

He led Theodore back past Mrs. West's office. At the end of the hall was the door to the outside, to a whole new world, a world beyond the workhouse that Theodore could not remember seeing before. The porter opened it for him, and a blast of winter air assaulted him, fresh and cool and exciting.

At the threshold, Theodore paused, glancing back towards Mrs. West's office. He would never see her again, he realized. The matron who had presided over his entire childhood would never again direct her ferocious glare at him.

He knew he should be excited, overjoyed at the thought, yet a strange sorrow touched him now. For the first time, Theodore wondered why it was that Mrs. West was so cruel. He wondered if life had beaten and crushed her into the monster she had become. Today, she had almost seemed kind.

"Are you coming?" barked the gardener.

Theodore turned, smiling. "Yes, sir!" he said, and walked out of the workhouse for the last time and into the crisp December air.

* * * *

It seemed as though Holly's limbs were composed of lead. She stumbled down the street, the heavy handcart rattling behind her, seeming to weigh as much as a house.

As much as the whole world.

Exhaustion had poured sand into her eyes, and she kept pausing to rub them as she waited for crossings to open up so that she could take a few more steps towards home.

It had been midnight last night before Holly finally finished washing that sheet, and was finally able to curl up beside Peggy's cot and attempt a few fitful snatches of sleep. Yet sleep was almost impossible.

Peggy kept crying out in her fever dreams, and no matter how Holly bathed her arms and legs with lukewarm water, the old woman's fever would not break.

Around her, the air was festive, and the smells of cinnamon and roasting chestnuts floated through the occasional open window.

Even though it was only the tenth of December, a few people were putting up wreaths on their doorways already. In just a little less than two weeks, it would be Christmas, and the air was filled with the promise of joy to come.

But Holly's heart felt like the empty hallways of the workhouse. Cold and dark and wailing with wind.

She tugged the handcart forward, stumbling across the cobblestones, praying with all of her heart that Peggy would still be alive when she reached home.

This morning, the money was almost finished. There was no more food, and no more medicine.

Holly had had no choice but to leave Peggy, shivering with fever upon her cot, and venture out into the world to take the laundry to its owners and gather a few pennies.

The thought of returning to a cottage devoid of life blew through Holly like a cold, cold wind. She shuddered with it and stumbled onwards.

She stumbled at last up to number thirteen and paused at the door, staring sightlessly at their neighbour's door. They had just hung a wreath of their own; it was all bright colours, green leaves, red holly, yellow ribbon. Peggy would love to see it. If Peggy was still alive.

Tears pooled behind Holly's eyes. With a tremendous effort, she swallowed them back, pushed open the door, and stepped into the cottage.

At once, she realized that there was light in here. The fire was burning merrily, even though it had been hours since Holly had left the cottage. She whipped around, handcart forgotten, and saw that Peggy was sitting up in her chair by the fire, sipping some tea, colour returning to her cheeks.

"Peggy!" Holly sobbed out. She rushed across the floor and flung her arms about the old woman's shoulders, hugging her tightly.

"Oh, stop your fuss, child," grumbled Peggy.

"Oh, Peggy, you're so much better," Holly sobbed, clinging on. "I – I was so afraid that – that you – "

"It'll take a little more than that to kill a stubborn old goat like me," croaked Peggy.

She began to cough, and Holly stepped back, cupping her hands around the old woman's where they gripped her tea.

"I brought food," Holly gushed, "and medicine."

Peggy's eyes widened, still watery with sickness. "How? How did we have any money?"

"I took washing up to the Petersen's."

"The Petersen's! But they sent us so much! How was it all done?"

Holly smiled through tears that were splashing down her cheeks. "I did it."

"Holly!" Peggy gaped at her, and then for the first time reached out and wrapped a skinny old arm around Holly's shoulders, hugging her close. "All on your own?"

"I had to," Holly sobbed, but this time she was crying with joy. "I had to buy medicine and food for you."

"Oh, Holly…" Peggy held her tightly for a few moments, coughing until she trembled. "I'll be all right, child," she whispered weakly. "I'll be all right."

"I brought some more medicine," said Holly. She produced it from her pocket and held it out. "It'll help for your cough, the apothecary said."

"Thank you, child." Peggy took it and gratefully sucked down a few sips.

Holly sank down at her feet, her head resting on Peggy's knees. "I'm just glad you're getting better. I thought…" Her voice trailed off.

"Don't think such things." Peggy patted the top of Holly's head with a gnarled, bony hand. "How much money do we have left?"

Holly shrugged a shoulder and looked at the floor. "I used it all, even the rent money. I'm sorry Peggy."

"Oh." Peggy sighed. "I'm the one that's sorry, Pet. I was really hoping for that roast chicken and those potatoes for you this Christmas, but we'll have to be sure to pay the rent first."

"I don't care about any of that." Holly flung her arms around Peggy's legs and buried her face in her lap. "I only want you."

"Tsk! Stupid child," muttered Peggy. But the hand that stroked Holly's hair was the most gentle touch that Holly had ever felt.

Chapter Seven

It was an usually sunny day for late December, and Holly was singing to herself as she folded the newly iron laundry and laid it in large, clean bags. There was still a week to go before Christmas, but she allowed the carol to come bubbling up in her chest and burst out of her full of joy.

"I saw three ships come sailing in on Christmas Day, on Christmas Day," she sang. "I saw three ships come sailing in on Christmas Day in the morning!"

She folded the last item of clothing and drew the bag shut, then hoisted it onto the little handcart in the laundry room. With a rattle of wheels, she drew the cart out of the laundry room and into the cottage, heading for the front door.

"I'm on my way out, Peggy!" Holly called.

Peggy looked up from the kitchen table. She had been busy reading a letter; Holly supposed it must have been a very long letter, as Peggy had been poring over it since after breakfast, almost an hour ago.

The old lady set the letter down and smiled, although Holly thought that some of the lines around her eyes seemed troubled.

"Are you going to see your friend today, do you think?" Peggy asked.

Holly smiled. "I hope so. It would be very nice to see Caroline, and I'm passing by the same park. It's a nice day, so I suppose she'll be outside."

"You two get along well, don't you?" said Peggy.

"I mean, she's very well to do, and I'm just a washerwoman's assistant." Holly smiled. "But she's been very nice to me, and we do really enjoy talking every time I go past there."

"That's good. Everyone should have friends." Peggy rose from the table. "You know, Holly, I think I'll walk with you today."

Holly hesitated. "It's quite far, Peggy, and you're not quite well yet. You don't want to get the fever again."

"I'm well enough to know my own mind, I should think," sniffed the old lady. "Besides, the doctor said that I needed fresh air and sunshine – and like you said, it's a lovely day."

Holly wasn't sure that the doctor had meant walking such a way, when he'd told Peggy she needed fresh air and sunshine, but she was also certain that there was no way she could stop Peggy when she had that look in her eye.

She told herself that she would simply have to keep the pace as slow as she could.

They set off, and for a few minutes neither of them spoke, both simply revelling in the glory of a sunny December day just a week before Christmas.

The bright sunshine brought every detail and colour into sharp relief: the colourful bunting hanging in the windows, the bright ribbons on the Christmas trees in people's homes and gardens, the shimmering baubles hanging on lamp-posts. Holly couldn't help singing again as she dragged the handcart onwards. Peggy was well, and it was a perfect, perfect day.

Still, as they neared the pretty district where Caroline's park was, Holly began to think that Peggy was being altogether too quiet. She glanced over at the old woman, worried. Peggy seemed to be walking comfortably, and she was barely coughing at all today, but her brow was wrinkled as though with worry.

"Is everything all right, Peggy?" Holly asked.

Peggy glanced over at her. "Yes, of course." She gave a small cough. "Why?"

"You're awfully quiet, that's all," said Holly. "And you seem a little upset about something."

"Codswallop," said Peggy. "Look at this lovely day. Everything is fine, child."

Holly knew better than to argue. They went on, and Peggy seemed to brighten up considerably. She pointed out the beautiful decorations in the well-off homes they were passing now: wreaths on all the doors, and gigantic Christmas trees in the windows, all hung with baubles and oranges, or angels shimmering at their tips.

They neared the park, and Holly looked around eagerly for Caroline as they approached the gate. She was not disappointed. Caroline was sitting on the usual bench near the gate, her hat in her lap, soaking in the rays of sunshine that made her hair shine more prettily than ever.

"Hello, Caroline!" Holly called softly, glancing around for Caroline's governess. The governess, however, seemed to have given up on trying to tell Caroline what to do. She was sitting on another bench a little way off, reading a book, and did nothing worse than scowl at Holly as she approached.

Caroline jumped to her feet, beaming. "Holly! It's lovely to see you." She bounded over to her. "And this must be Peggy! I'm so glad you're well. Holly tells me you were very ill."

"I was, but now I'm not," grunted Peggy.

"Peggy, this is Caroline." Holly put a hand on the old lady's shoulder.

Peggy nodded. "Charmed."

"I suppose I won't see you again until after Christmas, Holly." Caroline leaned on the gate in a highly unladylike fashion. "Ugh! It's going to be such a bore."

"Oh, but Christmas is so wonderful!" said Holly brightly. "There are going to be carollers going up and down the street all evening. Peggy and I like to go to the market square to listen to them."

"That part's all right. The food, too. I rather like roast goose, and plum pudding is my favourite." Caroline groaned. "It's just that Papa always invites all the stuffiest relatives to our house at Christmastime. They carry on so about the weather and politics and business and a whole lot of other things that I really can't care less about."

Holly blinked. She'd never tasted a roast goose before, not to think of plum pudding. Perhaps she'd be willing to put up with a few stuffy relatives if she could taste a little of Caroline's Christmas dinner.

"And my father gave us dreadfully boring presents last year." Caroline flicked the end of her long, thick braid over her shoulder. "Old books that bored me to death. Pah! If only he'd listened and brought me the hat that I asked for." She paused. "Then again, Holly, I suppose your Christmases are much poorer than mine, so perhaps I shan't complain."

"Oh, I don't think so." Holly smiled. "You may have nicer meals and even presents, but I think Christmas Eve in the market square is lovely."

Peggy cackled. "Don't be a fool, Holly. Why, I'd give up the market square for plum pudding any day!"

Caroline laughed merrily, her laugh as pure as silver sleigh bells. "Oh, you *are* funny, Peggy."

Peggy put her head a little to one side. "Caroline, do you live nearby?"

"Yes, we do. That's why I can come to the park every day." Caroline laughed. "Our house is at number four, Chestnut Street."

"That is not far at all," said Peggy thoughtfully.

A church bell tolled distantly, and Holly touched Peggy's arm. "We'd better be going, or we'll be late for our delivery."

"Of course." Peggy turned. "Goodbye, Caroline. And Merry Christmas to you."

"Merry Christmas!" Caroline called after them, and her voice was as pure as the voice of an angel.

* * * *

It was just two days before Christmas, and the sunshine was all gone.

Holly thrust her free hand into the pockets of her tattered dress against the biting wind that howled down the street, clutching the garment bag over her shoulder. Perhaps they wouldn't go to see the carollers tomorrow on Christmas Eve after all, she thought, not if the weather was like this.

It wouldn't feel quite the same without the little slices of fruit cake they usually bought—having saved up for months—to eat while they sat near the Christmas tree and listened to the songs. She would just buy some bread and cheese as usual, and they would eat together and have an early night. Peggy's recovery was all the Christmas she needed for this year.

Despite the cold that sought to plunge its little daggers through every piece of exposed flesh that it could find, and despite the hunger in her belly and the prospect of a quiet Christmas Eve, Holly's heart was light within her as she strode toward the house she would be delivering the laundry to.

Peggy was well, and she was well. It was all she could hope for. Christmas cakes were nothing in comparison.

There was only one thing she would ask for this Christmas, if she could, and it was Theodore.

Her heart squeezed in her chest at the thought of her one true friend. Theodore. He had always been so kind, his words so gentle.

She wished she could know what had become of him.

She wished she could see him just one more time, and thank him for being the voice in the darkness, when the darkness had threatened to swallow her whole.

Reaching a crossroads, Holly looked up, and her imagination must have been playing tricks on her, for she could swear that Theodore himself was walking along the pavement just across the street from her, heading across her field of vision. Of course, it couldn't be. She hadn't seen him in years, after all; he would be grown now, and there was no way she would recognize him.

Yet the sprightly step of the lad she saw in front of her, and the way he tucked his hands into his pockets and even the edges of the black curls rippling over his collar—they were all so familiar. Holly stood completely rooted to the spot for a few seconds.

Perhaps she would have stood there forever, and never known who it was that passed before her, if it was not for the fact that the boy suddenly stopped.

He looked this way and that, as though hearing something, like his name being called from afar or the strain of a beautiful piece of music borne on the cold wind. Holly opened her mouth, but no words came. For when the boy turned and she saw his face, she knew him at once.

It was Theodore.

A few moments dragged by, and Holly, torn by the wind, still couldn't move. Her heart beat wild wings against the bars of her ribs. Oh, there was no mistaking him. His cheeks and nose were pinched red with the cold and he wore a thick jacket and a wool scarf and hat pulled high on his chin, and low on his forehead, instead of the ugly workhouse stripes in which Holly knew him, but it was Theodore. She would know those eyes anywhere, and they lit up when they found hers. He knew her, too.

"Theodore!" Holly cried, and ran across the street pell-mell with her arms held out.

Theodore spun around and caught her in a tight embrace, hugging her the way he used to do when they were tiny children meeting in a dark hallway. She'd only ever really seen him at a distance or in mostly darkness, but here he was, in the daylight, on the outside of that dreaded place, laughing as he stepped back and grinned down into her face.

"Holly, it's you!" he said. "It's really you!"

Holly clutched his mittened hands with hers. "How?" she stammered. "How did you find me?"

"I didn't find you," said Theodore. "I—I live nearby now."

"Nearby?" Holly gasped, looking him up and down. His clothes were nice, but were they *that* nice?

"Oh, not in one of the houses, not in that way." Theodore smiled. "I'm an assistant gardener. I've only been here two weeks. I was sold from the workhouse."

"You've been in the workhouse all this time?" Holly asked, her heart squeezing.

"Yes, but now I'm free, and it's wonderful. The people I work for are a little troublesome at times, but nothing compared to Mrs. West." Theodore laughed. "And I have a half-day off on Sundays! I can do as I please. I'm on an errand now, though. Do you work here too?"

"Well, not far from here." Holly's eyes filled with happy tears. "I'm living with a kind washerwoman... working for her. I make deliveries here several days a week. Oh, Theo, I can see you often! I can see you every time I walk by if you give me your address!"

"Holly!" Theodore squeezed her hands. "It's a Christmas miracle. It's really a Christmas miracle!"

Holly smiled up at him, her heart wild in her chest. "Where do you live?"

"Number eight, Chestnut Street."

"I deliver laundry to number four." Holly laughed. "I really will see you often. Oh, Theo, you're right. It *is* a Christmas miracle!"

She went home laughing, wondering how many miracles could possibly fit into a single Christmas.

* * * *

Holly was singing at the top of her lungs when she burst into the kitchen. "Peggy, you won't believe what—" She stopped dead, the door slamming shut behind her on a gust of wind, and an eerie chill ran through her, like a candle being blown out in her spirit. "Peggy, what's the matter?"

Peggy was sitting at the table again, holding a letter, different from the previous one that she'd received last week. She lowered it slowly, looking up at Holly, and pushed out the chair beside her with one foot.

"Sit down, child," she said.

Holly was trembling. She went over to the table and set down the parcel of cheese and the loaf of bread she'd bought, then folded her hands in her lap, trying to hide their shaking.

"What's happening?" she whispered. "Are you all right?"

"Not really, Holly." Peggy took a deep breath. "But that's not what this letter is about. Actually, this letter is very, very good news."

"Good news?" Holly frowned. "Then why do you look so sad?"

Peggy sat back. "I've found you a job."

Holly's stomach lurched. "But I have a job... here, with you."

"Not anymore." Peggy reached over the table and wrapped a hard, bony hand around Holly's.

"What?" Holly's eyes burned with tears. "Have I done something wrong? Have I—"

"No!" Peggy snapped. "No. You've done everything right." The old lady's voice cracked, and she looked away. "You've been the child I've always wished for." She swallowed.

"Then why are you sending me away?"

"Because *I* have to go away."

Holly felt her tears spill over. "I don't understand."

"Let me begin at the beginning." Peggy straightened. "The first time I could venture out again, after the fever, I bumped into the apothecary in the market square."

Holly nodded. The apothecary had been the one who'd given her the medicine that saved Peggy's life.

"He told me that he was surprised to see me alive. That I have…" Peggy closed her eyes, flinching at the word. "Consumption."

"Oh, Peggy…" Holly felt her heart tumble into the great pit that opened suddenly in her stomach.

"My first thought was for you." Peggy stared at her. "I couldn't leave you helpless, and I want a better life for you than that of some old washerwoman."

"I love our life together."

"I know, but it's over now, and that's just a fact. The apothecary tells me I won't live another winter in London."

"Peggy!" Holly wailed.

"Don't fuss now, dear. I've finally given up." Peggy sighed. "I wrote to my sister. If I can be in the country air, perhaps I'll have a few more peaceful years… and I suppose the time has come for me to be with my family. She wrote back. She wants me to take the train to their place tomorrow morning."

"Tomorrow," Holly croaked, trying to swallow her tears.

"It's the only train there will be until after Christmas, since tomorrow is the twenty-third. Oh, Holly, I wanted you to come. I did." Peggy sighed. "But my sister can only take me. So… I found a job for you instead, but you'll love it. Oh, darling, try to look cheerful. It's a step up in the world for you."

Holly dragged a grubby sleeve over her face and summoned a smile. For Peggy, she would put a brave face on anything she had to. "I'm glad you're going to your sister," she said, meaning it. "You'll be happy there."

Peggy managed a crooked smile. "And you'll be happy in your new job, too. You're going to be a maid at Caroline Mills' house."

Holly felt a jolt of hope despite herself. "A maid?" She'd never dared to hope she would have such a high position. "Oh, Peggy, how did you—?"

"After I found out Caroline's address from her, I went there the next day, when you were delivering laundry further downtown," said Peggy. "The housekeeper wouldn't see me at first, but I kept it at. I told the housekeeper that you're the most hardworking, kindest, most willing girl I've ever met, and that she'd be a fool not to take you. Turns out they were quite desperate, especially with Christmas coming." She forced a smile. "You're friends with Caroline, aren't you? It'll be nice. You'll see her every day, and even do some duties caring for her rooms perhaps."

Holly's heart thudded in her chest. *Number eight, Chestnut Road*. It was just two doors down from Caroline's house. She would be able to see Theodore every single day.

"When?" Holly asked.

Peggy sighed. "You're to report to their house tonight."

"Tonight!" Holly gasped, the tears starting to well up again. "But... but then I almost have to leave... and I'll never see you again."

"That's the way of the world, child," said Peggy. She pushed away from the table and clumped off across the room, but Holly could hear her sobbing as she went.

* * * *

Holly could still feel the pressure of Peggy's last hug as she trudged up the long, slippery servants' path to the back door of the Mills' house.

She drew her shawl more tightly around her shoulders, wishing it would echo the pressure of the old lady's bony arms around her. She didn't think Peggy had ever embraced her before, but tonight, on the threshold of the cottage, she had held Holly as though she would never let go.

But let go she had, and now Holly was walking up to her new life, with everything she owned in a small laundry bag in her hands.

A spare jacket, a hat, and a piece of notepaper with Peggy's new address written on it. At least, Peggy said it was her new address. Holly had spent her lesson time in the workhouse the way she had spent all of her time there; cowering in fear from the bullies. She had never learned to read.

She trudged up to the back door and knocked nervously. It swung open to reveal a stern-faced housekeeper, her sagging jowls offset by a nose that jutted from the centre of her face like a poison arrowhead. "What do you want?" she barked.

"Please, ma'am," Holly stammered, "I'm the new maid."

The housekeeper regarded her for a few more seconds before widening the door.

"Hurry, then," she barked. "You're needed at once."

Holly scurried into a small kitchen that doubled as a servants' hall, with a narrow little table in the middle. It was largely empty now, but only four places were set.

Butler, housekeeper, maid, footman, Holly thought to herself.

She'd heard of larger households (it was no wonder this one needed a washerwoman's services since it had just one housemaid) but it still seemed amazing to her that one human being—presumably the father of the house—could support his family and four more people.

"I'll show you to your room," barked the housekeeper, "and you must change right away, then get to work."

The housekeeper shepherded her up a thin staircase to the servants' quarters. Holly's room was at the very end of a dark hallway, and when she pushed the door open, a familiar chill crept down between her shoulder blades.

"Be quick," the housekeeper snapped. "Put down your things and change into your uniform. You're needed in the kitchen."

She stamped out of the room, leaving Holly to stare at it. There was something very much like the workhouse about this room, even though it contained only one bed. The bed was as narrow as one of the workhouse bunks, and some cheap, rough linen was folded at its feet. A small trunk was pushed up against the opposite corner, and that was all. The room was utterly bare.

At least, in one way, it crucially differed from the workhouse dormitory. It had a window. A small window, to be sure, but it was right over the bed.

Holly went over to the bed, setting her bag down upon it, and peered through the window. She could just see the left wing of the house if she craned her neck, allowing her to look through the drawing-room window.

A Christmas tree was set up there, and the windows glowed with candles and bunting, mistletoe and holly. It seemed so strange that Christmas seemed only to exist for the family that owned the house and not for the people who worked within it.

Kneeling on the hard mattress, Holly rested her forehead against the cold glass and closed her eyes, an overwhelming wave of longing for Peggy washing over her. Peggy had shared everything she had with Holly. Christmas had permeated the very air of that cottage, even when there was only a bit of chicken and potatoes for Christmas Eve dinner.

She gave herself only a moment to stare before squeezing herself quickly into the uniform, struggling to tie the bow of the starched white apron behind her back. She'd washed so many of these uniforms before; she'd never imagined she would wear one someday.

A distant sound caught her attention: cheerful whistling, to the tune of "Joy to the World". Holly turned around and looked out of the window, and her heart turned a slow cartwheel in her chest. She could see over the wall of the Mills' garden, and all the way over the garden at number six next door, into the garden of number eight on the other side. It was from this garden that the sound of the whistling came.

A smile tugged at Holly's lips. Theodore was walking jauntily down the back garden, the ends of his scarf blowing in the wind, his whistling filling the air with pure joy. The sight of him flooded her heart with what felt like golden candlelight.

Theodore was Christmas miracle enough for her this year.

* * * *

On Christmas Eve, the next day, Holly crouched down on her hands and knees, scrubbing the wooden floor with all of her strength. An ugly wine-stain spread across the floorboards, splashed there a few minutes earlier by one of the guests, and the housekeeper had said that Mr. Mills would be furious if he rose from his Christmas Eve dinner with his guests to find the floor still stained. So she scrubbed with all her might, the brush hissing on the wood, her shoulders aching.

She thought of Christmas Eve with Peggy. Of walking to the market square to listen to the carollers, and eating sticky buns under the Christmas tree. Peggy had said that this would be a better life, but she wasn't so sure.

The dining hall door was open just a crack, and the sight beyond was a splendid one. Caroline and her two parents were sitting at a long, beautiful table, along with a party of relatives.

The table was laden with food the likes of which Holly had only ever dreamed of: stuffed goose, mounds of roast vegetables, plum pudding, fruit cakes, oranges, roasted chestnuts, soft white buns, whole dishes of golden butter.

Garlands and mistletoe were arranged tastefully on the table and draped from every surface, with enormous red and green and yellow satin bows tied at the corners of the table. A Christmas tree towered in the corner of the room, all decked out with ribbons and baubles and, with a golden star glittering brightly at the top. Parcels wrapped in ribbon and paper were piled deeply at its feet.

Caroline was eating the last of her plum pudding in delicate little bites, flashing her bright smile at her relatives. She looked radiant with her golden hair piled on top of her head, making her look very grown-up even though she was only about fourteen herself.

When the butler had cleared away the plates and the master rose to his feet to retire to the drawing-room, Holly sucked in a breath, quickly wiping a cloth over the floor a last time and dumping the brush into the bucket. She was in the motion of scurrying away when the dining hall door opened and the master stepped into the hallway.

"You!" he barked. "You're the new maid, are you not?"

Holly kept her eyes downcast and nodded

The master merely grunted, then strode away.

Caroline gave her a quick grin as she followed her father to the drawing-room, and it gave Holly a brief flicker of courage. Maybe things would be all right. Maybe she would be happy here, eventually, since Caroline was her friend.

Part Three

Chapter Eight

Four Years Later

The Rochester's, tonight's guests at the Mills house, were far wealthier than the Mills, and Caroline had dressed accordingly.

Resplendent in a sky blue dress that glimmered with embroidery and glittering beads, she moved around the floor with effortless grace, her white shoulders shining in the light of the grand chandeliers hanging from the ceiling.

Only the most modest amount of powder and rouge had been applied to her face, making them glow slightly more from the exertion as she waltzed so lightly that it appeared she was floating, the hems of her many petticoats brushing the polished wood of the floor with the lightest touch.

Holly smiled from the back of the room where she stood at the ready of the Butler's orders, as Caroline and her partner swept past.

The young man wore a navy-blue suit with long, elegant tails that perfectly complemented Caroline's dress, and his wonderful head of thick golden curls bobbed slightly as he whisked her across the ballroom. Across the room, Holly could see Caroline's father watching with satisfaction.

It would be something indeed if middle-class Caroline Mills married an heir like Adam,. The Mills were no longer quite so middle-class as they had been four years ago when Holly had first come to work there.

They were a slightly larger household now, with three maids, although Caroline had never been able to keep a lady's maid. Holly could only be grateful that she hadn't been stuck as a scullery-maid, but could work as a housemaid instead now.

Sighing with relief that the evening was going to plan for the Mills ball, Holly glanced around the room to check that everything was in place.

Normally, the Mills parlour was quite modest, though its furniture had been upgraded last year. But today, for their Christmas party, it shone with Christmas decorations.

The deep green garlands that hung all around the room were punctuated by wreaths, wrapped in bright red ribbons that neatly matched the holly berries on each one. A Christmas tree stood in the corner of the room, alight with shining gold and silver baubles.

There was a Nativity scene, too, with bright candles shining all around the wise men as they bowed before the manger. Holly could not quite see the face of the statue of the Babe that lay within it.

She was gazing at the Nativity scene when Caroline and Adam swept past her once more, and there was a sudden, sharp crack. Caroline stumbled—a movement that seemed incongruous for such a graceful form—and cried out, coming to a halt.

"Dear Caroline!" cried Adam. "What's the matter?"

"Oh, I'm so clumsy. You must forgive me." Caroline's cheeks deepened to bright red. "The heel of my shoe has broken."

Holly had already darted out from behind the curtain, keeping her head down as Adam led Caroline off the dance floor, supporting her on one arm as she limped dramatically. As Caroline sank onto a chair nearby, Holly stepped up beside her. "Are you hurt, miss?"

Caroline shot her a quick look. "No, I'm all right. Run and bring me shoes from my room."

"Of course, miss." Holly ran upstairs, grabbed a pair of dancing shoes from the closet and was back in the parlour in a trice, offering Caroline the shoes.

"Well, aren't you an attentive little lady's maid," laughed Adam.

Holly avoided his gaze as she crouched down and slipped off Caroline's shoes.

"Oh, she's not my lady's maid. Just a housemaid—my lady's maid is indisposed today," Caroline sniffed.

Holly knew that the last lady's maid had just been fired after Caroline had told her father that the hapless girl had pulled her hair too much when she was brushing it.

Again, she felt a pang of relief that she was far too common to end up with that particular role.

Caroline smiled at Adam. "I'm so sorry we couldn't finish the waltz."

"Oh, not at all." Adam laughed lightly. "I needed a little breather, at any rate."

Holly glanced up at him. His eyes were upon her, piercingly green, and she looked away quickly as she slid one of the dancing slippers onto Caroline's left foot.

"I'm amazed that you had no need even to call for a maid. She is a credit to your household." Adam smiled, but Holly knew he was still watching her.

"Oh, the Butler trains his staff very well," sniffed Caroline. "Do hurry up, Holly."

"It must be a pleasure to have her attend you," said Adam. "And you must enjoy working for the Mills, too, don't you?"

Holly nodded, knowing better than to say anything. Her cheeks were flushing at the inappropriateness of Adam's attention upon her.

"Adam, don't let's talk about servants now." Caroline laughed. "You were telling me about your journey to Paris last year."

"Oh, was I?" Adam asked, but did not go on.

Holly glanced up at him again as she slid on the second slipper. He was watching her, a faint smile curling her lips, and the way his eyes slithered over her body as she straightened up made goosebumps rise upon her skin.

Caroline's blue eyes were boring into her. Holly had to muster all of her courage to ask, "Will that be all, miss?"

"Yes, that will certainly be all," Caroline snapped.

Holly curtsied hurriedly and fled back to the kitchen, her heart pounding. As she darted out of the room, she could still see Adam looking at her over Caroline's head, that same smile playing upon his lips.

* * * *

Caroline's silence stalked through the room like a hunting cat. Holly could feel its silent paws padding across the thick carpet as she turned down the bed, hear its soft growl as it came closer and closer, feel its whiskers brushing against her calves as she laid out Caroline's nightgown.

Not a word was spoken as Caroline came into the room and retreated behind her screen to dress while Holly stoked the fire. And all the while, the silence surrounded them, and Holly's stomach knotted more and more tightly.

Even here in Caroline's room, Christmas decorations festooned every surface. A bright stocking hung over the mantelpiece, which was draped with mistletoe and in which leaped a warm golden fire. There was a wreath on the door and a brightly coloured Christmas card on her dresser. Yet Caroline's brow was knotted as furiously as though none of the finery around her made any difference to her.

The girl finally spoke when she stepped out from behind her screen, and her voice was dangerously low, trembling with emotion.

"What did you think you were doing?"

Holly looked up. The haughty older girl's cheeks were glowing red with fury.

"Excuse me, miss?" Holly whispered.

Caroline's gaze hardened in the mirror. "You know full well what I'm talking about, Holly. Don't play the fool with me. I saw you watching Adam Rochester."

Holly looked away, her heart sinking. Things had been so different ever since Caroline turned sixteen two years ago and her father had begun to consider her old enough to find a suitor—preferably a well-off, well-bred one who would elevate the Mills name from middle-class to upper-class.

"Please, miss, I didn't watch him," she murmured.

Caroline slammed a hand down on her vanity, rattling the jars and bottles upon it with the force of the blow. "Nonsense!" she shrieked. "Nonsense! Nonsense! Nonsense!"

Holly cringed, her heart fluttering in her chest. "Please, miss, I don't..."

"You know what you did!" Caroline screamed at her. "I had Adam eating from the palm of my hand until *you* walked in and tried to charm him with your big brown eyes and your sweet little smile!"

Holly backed away, her heart thumping. "I just wanted to bring you your slippers, miss."

"You're always like this," cried Caroline. "You always want to seduce my suitors even though you're just a common little ragamuffin girl who means nothing!"

Holly had to blink away the hot tears that rushed to her eyes. "I don't want to seduce anyone, miss. I just wanted to bring you your slippers like you asked me to do."

"Don't you understand? Adam is *mine*," Caroline hissed. "I'm going to marry him, and he's going to make me rich, and I'm going to be Mrs. Caroline Rochester, heiress to a fortune. I'm going to do as my papa says and make him proud." Her eyes narrowed. "And you will only ever be a stupid, lonely, pointless little housemaid with no purpose in life. You will only ever be nothing."

This time, a tear escaped down Holly's cheek. "Oh, Caroline," she whispered. "We used to be friends. What happened?"

Caroline's face twisted with fury. "That's Miss Mills to you, maid," she barked. "Now finish with the fire. Just do your job!"

Holly's hands were shaking as she turned back to the fire. She dared to look at Caroline only one more time as she fled the room, and it was to see Caroline's eyes staring back at her, their shining depths filled with an emotion she had not expected.

It was fear.

* * * *

The housekeeper at the Clifford's' home had given Theodore a leftover bit of holly for his buttonhole, and he could just catch glimpses of its bright red berries as he strode towards the park, humming "O Come All Ye Faithful" as he went.

They gleamed dully in the veiled sunlight; the clouds were low and grey, and snow crunched beneath Theodore's feet as he went, but nothing could dim the light and joy burning through his heart. For it was a Sunday afternoon, and that meant, as it had done for the past four years, that it was time to visit with Holly.

When he reached the gate of the park, she was already waiting for him. She had changed out of her black-and-white uniform and was wearing the plain green linen dress that she had been so proud to buy with her own savings last year, when she had hopelessly outgrown the old dress as new curves had developed in her growing body.

Theodore's eyes, however, did not touch the perfect shapeliness into which she had grown in the past few years. He looked only at her face, at the way her brown eyes lit up when she smiled, at the glow in her cheeks when she saw him coming and rose from the park bench down by the frozen duck pond.

"Theo!" she called to him, her voice music upon the air.

Theodore strode over to her, laughing, holding out his arms. She rushed into them, and he spun her in a circle, delighting at the feeling of her heart fluttering against his chest.

He lowered her to the ground and smiled down at her, basking in the glow of her beauty: her great brown eyes so dark and filled with mystery, her torrent of black hair pouring down her back, the roundness of her cheeks and the deep dimples left there by the smile that lit up his universe.

"I've been waiting all week for this moment," Theodore said, because it was the only thing he could make himself do rather than draw her close and kiss her.

"You always say that." Holly giggled, the laugh more melodic than any carol. "I brought some cheese."

Theodore let her go, patting his pocket. "And I brought ham sandwiches."

"Ham sandwiches!" Holly smiled. "Mrs. Goodwin really does like you."

"Mrs. Goodwin is a good soul. She likes everyone." Theodore led her over to the bench, touching the sprig of holly in his buttonhole. "She gave me this, too."

They sat down together, and Holly touched the sprig, her fingertips lightly brushing his chest. "It's very pretty. The Mills' house is full of holly now, too."

Theodore took out the sandwiches and unwrapped them, giving one to Holly. "The Clifford's' have been a little late this year, but they've started putting up their decorations now, too. About time, considering Christmas Eve is next week! I've been tending those holly bushes all year, and now they have more berries than any other bushes on the street."

"I saw your mistletoe over the fence yesterday, too." Holly smiled as though it was the most magical thing she had ever seen. "It's beautiful! And so big."

"Simon says it's never been as big as it is this year." Theodore smiled. "He's taught me so much. I feel sorry for him this winter, though. The rheumatic has been plaguing him dreadfully in this cold."

"Poor Simon." Holly sighed. "Do you think you'll be head gardener when he retires?"

"I know I'm very young for it, so perhaps not." Theodore shrugged. "The Clifford's might hire a more experienced gardener instead, but Simon has been talking about trying to get them to make me head gardener."

Holly beamed up at him. "Oh, Theo, won't that be wonderful?"

He could not resist leaning down and planting a delicate kiss upon her forehead. "It would be perfect in every way, Holly. I would have a cottage of my own… enough money for a family." His cheeks flushed with heat.

But Holly did not look away from his eyes. "That sounds perfect," she whispered.

He reached up, tracing a finger down the curve of her cheeks. She was the most wonderful thing he had ever seen. He didn't know how to put into words the glorious feeling in his heart whenever he laid eyes on her, but he did know that when he had that cottage someday, she would be the one to join him in it.

"Oh, I have some good news for you," he said, forcing himself to look away and take a bite of his sandwich.

"What is it?"

"The Mills have asked for some help cutting hothouse flowers and greens from their garden for their own Christmas Eve dinner." Theodore grinned. "I'll be coming over for a few hours next week to help your gardener, since you don't have an assistant gardener."

"Oh, that'll be lovely!" Holly grinned. "I'll be working, but it will be lovely to look out of the window and see you in the garden. You'll like our hothouse, too. It's very small, of course, but there are plenty of flowers in it."

"None of them are as pretty as you," said Theodore.

Holly giggled.

They ate their sandwiches slowly, watching as laughing children skated on the pond, racing each other, their skates spitting bits of ice as they spun and turned and raced off the other way again.

"I didn't see the Clifford's at the Mills' party last night," Holly said at length.

"Oh, no. The Clifford's are becoming more and more hermits each year, I'm afraid." Theodore laughed. "But I'm sure you were busy."

"Of course. It was a difficult evening. Caroline is determined as ever to marry Adam Rochester." Holly's face fell, and she lowered her sandwich back to her lap, as though she was losing her appetite.

Theodore draped an arm around her shoulders. "What's the matter?"

Holly sighed. "Caroline was in one of her rages last night."

Theodore squeezed her shoulders gently. "I'm sorry."

"She says such hurtful things, Theo. It's hard to believe that she and I used to be friends once." Holly blinked back tears.

"She said that I was seducing Adam. I didn't even look at him. I would never do such a thing."

"Caroline is just jealous because she's unlucky in love and you're much more beautiful than she is," said Theodore.

"Theo!"

"It's the truth, Holly. Look at you. You catch the attention of every man who passes by you... even Caroline's suitors. And she has never had steady attention from any single man, has she?"

Holly sighed. "Adam does dance with her at most of the balls, but he never calls at the house or writes to her."

"Exactly. He might like dancing with her, but he won't marry her, and she knows it." Theodore shrugged. "She knows that you're sweeter, kinder, and more beautiful than she is, and it makes her jealous."

Holly sighed, resting her head on his shoulder. "I think she's jealous of me because of you."

"Because of me?" Theodore laughed.

"Yes. Because I have something she doesn't—the love of a good man."

Theodore's heart swelled at her words, and he squeezed her a little more tightly. "You know, Holly," he said softly, "one day, you and I will always be together. We will never be parted. You won't have to be anyone's maid anymore, and we'll have Christmas in our own home together, with our own Christmas tree and our own wreaths and our own roast chicken for dinner."

Holly closed her eyes, sighing, a soft smile playing on her face. "That sounds perfect," she said again.

Chapter Nine

Holly thanked God for the gloriously sunny sky today. It meant that, instead of working in the silent and stuffy rooms of the house, she was outside polishing a wooden garden bench while Theodore worked away at the holly bushes just across the lawn.

The Mills gardener, Tommy, was a dour old man and communicated only in grunts, but Theodore was whistling as he worked. "Joy to the World", as usual. It was his favourite Christmas carol, too.

Caroline sat across Holly on another bench, turning a page in her book. The girl's studious face was gently rouged, as always, and a diamond necklace glittered at her throat in the shape of a star.

Holly quickly turned away from Caroline and worker harder at polishing her bench, hoping that Caroline would go back home soon. Her arm was beginning to cramp a little.

Across the lawn, Theodore cast a glance towards her, and their eyes met briefly.

Holly couldn't stop her lips from curling in a smile, which Theodore returned, his eyes sparkling with pleasure. She felt a blossom of excitement in the pit of her stomach and dropped her gaze back to her work.

Caroline huffed, closing the book and shooting Holly a furious look. "Must you do that?"

Holly blinked. "I beg your pardon, miss?"

"You know exactly what I'm talking about." Caroline glared towards Theodore. "If you must engage in scandalous relations during your own time, at least don't bring it into your work, too."

"Miss Caroline!" Holly gasped, the accusation a hot knife in her chest.

"I'm tired of this." Caroline slammed her book shut and swept to her feet. "I feel like a little turn about the garden. Come here, Holly, and give me your arm in case I slip on the snow."

"Yes, of course, miss." Holly set down her polishing things and held out an arm to Caroline, who grasped it with hard, cruel fingers, and began to lead her on a little walk around the garden.

The garden was not particularly large, but Caroline walked very slowly, especially once Theodore was out of sight. Holly did her best not to glance longingly over her shoulder toward him. Instead, she guided Caroline as carefully as she could, avoiding the icy spots on the garden path.

A silence hung between them, far colder than the snow that crunched beneath their boots.

Holly glanced up at Caroline's face, thinking of what Theodore had said about the fact that Caroline had never really had a beau. Many suitors, but never one that truly showed an interest in her beyond exploiting her excellent dancing skills. A pang of pity ran through her heart. Theodore was the cornerstone of her world, and she could only wonder how lonely Caroline felt, with her cold father and insipid mother.

"Are you excited for Christmas Eve, miss?" Holly asked softly.

Caroline scoffed. "Of course I am. Papa's Christmas Eve gathering is the finest on the entire street. I'm not sure it's altogether ladylike to be 'excited', as you put it, in any case."

Holly lowered her gaze, deciding to maintain the silence. They made their circuit of the lawn, passing by the hothouse and the holly bushes. Theodore gave Holly a secret little smile as they passed, and she felt a wonderful flutter of joy in the pit of her stomach when he did so.

Caroline let out a shriek. It tore through Holly's ears, making her jump.

"Miss! Miss, what is it?" Holly gasped, clutching Caroline's arm.

"My necklace!" Caroline screamed. "It's gone!"

Holly glanced at the neckline of Caroline's beautiful dress. Where the diamond star-shaped necklace had hung just a few moments ago, there was nothing. Her heart thudded. "You had it on a moment ago, when you were sitting on the bench."

"It must have fallen off!" Caroline's eyes filled alarmingly with tears. "We must find it. We *must*!"

Theodore had come over, his eyes concerned. "What's the matter?"

"I'm looking for my diamond necklace," Caroline sobbed. "Oh, please, help me find it!"

A pang of pity ran through Holly's gut. Caroline's father had given her that necklace last Christmas; she must have underestimated how much it meant to the girl. She squeezed Caroline's hand. "Don't worry, miss. Sit down and try to calm yourself. I'll find it, I promise."

"I'll help," said Theodore. "I'll follow your footprints around the garden and see if it's lying there somewhere."

"I'll look under the bench," said Holly.

"Oh, thank you, thank you." Caroline sank onto the bench, sobbing into both hands. "Thank you so much."

Holly got down on her hands and knees, ignoring the biting pain of the cold through her dress, and patted around on the snow beneath the bench. For once, she cursed the sunlight that made diamond and snow alike sparkle so brightly. Squinting against the white snow, she felt around for the delicate chain, for the tiny star-shaped diamond that had to be around her somewhere.

But even after Holly's knees were wet through from the snow, she still couldn't find it anywhere. Caroline was sobbing all the harder. "It's all right, miss," Holly said. "Theodore will find it. I know he will."

"Oh, he must, he must!" Caroline sobbed.

Theodore walked up to him, his face long, and shook his head. "I'm so sorry, miss. I can't see it anywhere. Are you sure it hasn't fallen under the bench?"

"I'm sure." Holly sighed, picking up Caroline's book and shaking out the pages, but there was no sign of the necklace.

"Oh, no, no, no!" Caroline wailed.

Holly put a hand on the girl's shoulder. "Come on, Miss Caroline, it'll be all right. It might have fallen—" She glanced at Theodore.

He caught her expression, smiling faintly, and gave a little bow. "I'll get back to my work now." He strode off.

Holly turned back to Caroline, squeezing her shoulder. "Miss Caroline, it might have just fallen into your bodice. I'm sure if you take off your dress we'll find it in there somewhere."

Caroline swiped at her running eyes, snivelling. "Yes... yes. Maybe. Oh, I hope so. Oh, Holly!"

"It's all right, miss." Holly helped her to her feet. "Come on. Let's see if we can find it."

She held Caroline's trembling hand tightly in her own as she led her back to the house.

* * * *

Theodore cast the last of his gardening tools into his wheelbarrow: the pruning shears and scissors he'd been using to cut and clean holly sprigs from the bushes around the Mills home. It had been strange to work under the Mills' gardener, a dour old man named Roberts who barked orders and never smiled. He was ready to be working with Simon again, yet there was one thing he would miss bitterly about helping the Mills.

A smile tugged at his lips as he looked back towards the house. It was evening, and the house was all lit up from the inside with gas lamps that sparkled upon the Christmas decorations he could see in every window.

Well, almost every window. One, small and square and set high up near the back of the house, was still dark and empty. Holly had pointed it out to him once. It was the window to her room.

He glanced at it often when he worked in the Clifford's' garden, but right now there was no cause to gaze longingly at the small glass pane. Instead, he smiled as a slim figure came down the servants' path towards him, clutching a candle in one hand even though the light above the servants' entrance cast a weak glow into the back garden.

"Are you leaving?" Holly asked softly, shielding the candle with one hand. Its flame cast dancing shadows over her soft, round cheeks.

"Yes, I'm afraid so." Theodore pulled off his heavy gloves and put them into the wheelbarrow. "But I'll see you tomorrow, Christmas Eve, when we meet in the park after supper like we said, won't I?"

"Of course." Holly's smile flickered, but it failed to reach her troubled eyes.

Theodore reached out and rested both hands on her shoulders. "Holly, what's the matter? Did you find Miss Caroline's necklace?"

"We didn't." Holly hung her head. "It must have fallen in the garden, Theo, but we searched everywhere for it. I've just been out there again now, searching, while Caroline and her family are at the supper table."

"I'm so sorry. Perhaps one of you accidentally trampled it into the snow," said Theodore. "Although I took a rake and turned all that snow over where you'd been walking to be sure."

"I know you did. It's not there." Holly covered her face with one hand. "I don't know where it could be. I just... I hope I don't get any blame."

"It's going to be all right, Holly." Theodore squeezed her shoulders. "Whatever happens, I'll be here for you."

"Thank you," Holly sobbed. "Thank you. I... I have to go."

"See you tomorrow?" Theodore smiled.

She nodded, a faint flicker of hope crossing her face. "See you tomorrow."

She headed back towards the house, and Theodore picked up his wheelbarrow and made his way the short distance down the street to the Clifford's' home.

Soft music was being played inside the house as Theodore passed by on his way to the garden shed. He paused, glancing through the drawing-room window.

The Clifford's were elderly, and it was one of their granddaughters sitting at the piano, a bright blue ribbon in the centre of her back, her fingers dancing over the keys as she drew forth the merry tune of "Hark the Herald Angels Sing".

"Glory to the new-born King!" Theodore sang to himself, taking his wheelbarrow back to the shed. When he returned to the servants' hall, Mrs. Goodwin was busy setting the table for supper.

"Look at you, boy!" the plump old woman said, gesturing at his grubby hands. "Go on and wash up before supper, there's a good lad."

"Thank you, Mrs. Goodwin." Theodore grabbed a chestnut from a bowl in the middle of the table, and she slapped at him half-heartedly with a napkin as he bounded up the stairs to his small room.

It was little more than a cubicle, and he shared it with a footman. There was barely any room to fit between the two beds, and there were no windows. Theodore turned on the gas lamp and rooted in his trunk for a towel. Before leaving for the washroom, however, he couldn't resist sitting down on his bed and reaching beneath his pillow.

A small, cold circle was lying there, and he drew it out into the light, turning it this way and that as he admired it. Of course, it was nothing compared to the glittering, bejewelled rings he had seen before.

This little ring was made only of iron, polished by the blacksmith, and he had already had to save every penny for two years to be able to afford it. He could only just slip it onto the first joint of his own pinkie finger, and he smiled down at it.

It wasn't much, but he could only imagine the look in Holly's eyes when he presented it to her tomorrow night after supper and asked her, someday, when the world was a better place, when he was head gardener, when there was a cottage and a little more money—when he asked her, at last, if she would someday become his wife.

* * * *

Holly cast nervous glances at Caroline as she turned down the bed. The girl sat at her vanity, slowly running a brush through her own thick golden tresses.

She had been very quiet all through her bath and getting dressed for bed as well. Despite the cruel words Caroline had spoken to Holly so often over the past two years, she could not help but to feel desperately sorry for her.

"I'll go looking for your necklace again at first light, miss," she said. "I'm sure it must be out there somewhere."

"Do you know, Holly…" Caroline sighed. "I don't think it is."

"What do you mean? It must be there somewhere."

"Unless someone took it." Caroline's words slammed like a closing door.

Holly's heart jumped. "But… but who would have taken it?"

Caroline raised her eyes to the mirror, and they were as cold as two chips of ice in her beautiful face. "I don't know, Holly. Who has recently come to work here that my family doesn't really know? Who was in the garden this morning when we took our little walk, and would have had plenty of opportunity to pick up the necklace if it had fallen by the bench?"

Holly froze in the middle of turning down the bed. She felt herself reeling with the terrible implication in her tone. "It wasn't Theodore," she spat out. "I know it wasn't. I know with all of my heart that it wasn't."

"So do I," said Caroline, looking down and smoothing the folds of her dress, but her next words quickly killed the faint spark of relief that had risen in Holly's chest. "I know exactly where that necklace is, but I also know that you and Theodore have been sweet on each other for years and years, when I can't even get a young man to look in my direction."

"What do you mean?" Holly stammered out. "Where is it?"

"I won't tell you. In fact, I won't tell anyone. That stupid necklace is as good as gone in any case. I hated it from the moment I saw it." Caroline's words dripped with venom. "Did you really think I would simply stand by and watch you be happy with Theodore when I've never had any luck in love, Holly?"

Holly could barely breathe. "Caroline, please…"

"My family's entire fate hinges on whether or not I can marry the right man," Caroline spat. "But you! *You* have that boy hanging on your every word without even trying. It's not fair, Holly. It's not fair, and I won't stand by and watch you like this while I suffer!"

Tears coursed down Holly's cheeks. "How can you say that?" she sobbed. "We're not hurting you. We're not doing anything improper. You're just jealous! Why would you hurt us because of your jealousy?"

"Because I can't have what you want!" Caroline cried. "And that hurts, Holly, oh, it hurts more than you could ever dream of!" She rose from her chair and turned to face Holly, and tears sparkled in her eyes. "Do you know how terribly lonely my life has become? Do you know how I long for what you have? I shan't let you have it if I can't. I shan't!"

"Please don't," Holly sobbed. "Please. Just leave Theodore and I be."

Caroline scoffed. "It's far too late for that, I'm afraid. It's all planned out." She gave Holly a long, level stare. "Tomorrow, before the Christmas Eve supper, you'll tell Papa that you saw Theodore take the necklace."

Holly's heart squeezed in her chest. No! Theodore would certainly be dismissed without any references. How would he ever find work again? He may even end up back in the workhouse, back with Mrs. West, with those long dark hallways, with the refractory ward...

"No!" she gasped, feeling as though that dread darkness she had avoided for eight years was pressing down upon her once more. "No, I won't!"

"Suit yourself," sniffed Caroline, tossing her hair. "Then I'll tell Papa that *you* took my necklace."

"I didn't," Holly cried. "You can't."

"Of course I can. Who do you think Papa will believe—me, or you?" Caroline glared at her.

Holly's heart fumbled within her. She couldn't lie about Theodore. But what would happen to her if Mr. Mills thought she'd taken the necklace? Dismissed. Alone. She would go back to the workhouse. Mrs. West, and the darkness—

"You have until tomorrow night to decide." Caroline sat back down in her chair. "Now finish with my bed."

Tears ran silently down Holy's cheeks as she turned back to the bed.

Chapter Ten

Holly was beginning to hope that Caroline had forgotten all about the necklace.

She slid the last pin into Caroline's hair, fixing up a last curl into the sumptuous pile on top of the girl's head. Aglitter with shining pins and bright ribbons, Caroline smiled at her reflection in the mirror. "Thank you, Holly," she said sweetly. "I just couldn't quite reach that one."

"Of course," said Holly. "It's my pleasure." She prayed silently that she could have another miracle this Christmas: that Caroline would never make good on her threat.

The girl certainly seemed to be in a good mood. She swept to her feet, her skirts rustling, and laughed as she twirled in the centre of her large room. She was wearing a beautiful yellow dress that flared as she spun, and there was another necklace, this time set with a small sapphire, hanging at her throat. "Papa will be so proud of me," she said. "Come now, Holly. Let's go downstairs."

"But miss, I have duties…" Holly began.

Caroline seized her wrist. "Downstairs," she said firmly, and dragged Holly out of the room and down the hallway.

Holly's blood pounded in her ears. Surely Caroline simply wanted Holly to attend her when they went down to the dining hall. Surely all would be well…

All was not well. Caroline did not go down to the dining hall. Instead, she turned sharply left on the ground floor and led Holly up to the heavy oak door that led to the drawing-room. She paused to listen for a moment, then smirked. "Mama isn't here. Good. She's always been a temperate influence on him."

"Caroline…" Holly whimpered.

Caroline knocked on the door. "It's me, Papa."

The butler opened it, and Caroline swept into the room, Holly borne helplessly in her wake. Mr. Mills was sitting by the fire, smoking a cigar, and he looked up as his daughter came in. The man's cold blue eyes swept up and down Caroline's figure, assessing her, before relaxing into a smile.

"Caroline, darling," he said. "Come and sit down. It's not quite time for supper yet."

"I know, Papa." Caroline kept a firm grip on Holly's wrist as she walked over to the settee opposite her father and sat. When she let go of Holly, she made a fuss over straightening out Caroline's skirts and then tried to retreat, but a single look from Caroline froze her in place.

"You do look lovely in that yellow satin, darling," said Mr. Mills. "But where is your diamond necklace? A sapphire isn't really suitable for this company, you know."

Holly had seen Mrs. Clifford wear sapphires plenty of times in public, and they were far more well-off than the Mills. Of course, she said nothing.

"That's why I'm here to talk to you, Papa." Caroline squared her shoulders. "Holly has something to tell you."

Holly's entire being cringed with fear when Mr. Mills looked up at her, his eyes narrowing. "You? The housemaid?"

"Sir…" Holly curtseyed hurriedly. "There's been a misunder—"

"Go on, Holly. Don't be shy." Caroline wore a triumphant smile. "Tell my father all about what you saw."

Mr. Mills leaned forward. "What did you see? And what does this have to do with the diamond necklace?"

Holly was shaking. She was trapped now. There was no way of getting out of this, not with Caroline's cold eyes so firmly fixed upon her, the look in them echoed in Mr. Mills'.

She had tossed and turned all night, and she knew what she had to say. She would tell the truth. She would say that she had seen nothing, that she knew nothing of the necklace's disappearance. She would say that it must have been lost.

And then Caroline would leap up, and accuse Holly of being the thief, of having taken it. And Mr. Mills would believe her. And Holly would be out on the street, in the darkness, that oppressive, stifling darkness that rushed into her and tried to suffocate her, the darkness that had almost killed her…

"Well?" barked Mr. Mills. "Spit it out, child."

Holly opened her mouth, and thought for a terrible moment she might vomit. She could feel the darkness crowding around the house, pressing down upon it, surrounding it. She thought of the refractory ward, of how she had thought she was dead.

She could never go back.

"The assistant gardener from the Clifford's' house," she was saying, though she barely heard herself utter the words. "I saw him take the necklace."

She knew what she had done the moment she said the words, and it was in that moment that the darkness rushed into her in a way it had never done before. Even though the firelight was leaping in the hearth and sparkling up on the baubles that hung from the windowsill and lighting up the brightly wrapped presents underneath the tree, Holly felt closer to the darkness than ever before. It was inside her now. In her heart. Where she had allowed it within her by uttering that single, hurtful, heinous lie.

Mr. Mills lunged to his feet. "That scoundrel!" he thundered. "That thief!"

"No!" Holly cried out, her heart ripped open. What had she done? What had she done?

Caroline stepped in front of her, silencing her. "Oh, Papa, you won't let him go unpunished, will you? You'll get my beautiful necklace back, won't you? I love it so much, and you gave it to me last year, for Christmas." She began to cry great, round, false tears.

"Of course I will, my darling." Mr. Mills bunched his hands into fists. "I shall send for the police at once. That boy will hang for this!"

Hang. The word fell into Holly's stomach like a great stone. Sweat prickled on her palms, on her forehead, and even Caroline stepped back, eyes widening. "Hang, Papa? You mean—be killed?"

"Of course. That's the punishment for theft, you know." Mr. Mills put an arm around Caroline's shoulders. "But don't worry about that now, my darling. Come in and have a lovely supper with us. You don't have to think about that awful boy anymore—and your necklace will soon be safe with you again."

Mr. Mills led her away, and as they reached the door of the drawing-room, Caroline gave her one glance back. Her eyes were huge and terrified and filling with real tears this time. But she said nothing. She admitted to nothing. She just went with her father to the dining hall, leaving Holly alone in the drawing-room, her heart filled with the realization of what she had done.

She was killing Theodore, the man that she loved.

* * * *

Theodore held up a small glass of the eggnog that Mrs. Goodwin had made. "To another year with you all," he said, "and to the glorious hope that Christmas has brought to the world!"

"Well said, young man!" grunted Simon, raising his glass to tap against Theodore's.

"And thank you, pet." Mrs. Goodwin smiled. "It was only cheap rum that the master gave me, but it was good of him to give us anything at all."

"The Clifford's are good folk," said Simon. "I'm grateful to be working for them."

Theodore nodded as he took a small sip of the eggnog, its spicy, creamy flavour sliding richly down his throat. He shifted in place as Mrs. Goodwin began to pile heaping servings of their modest but hearty Christmas Eve supper onto their plates: baked potatoes, some roast chicken, and a hearty rice pudding.

It was some of the best food he'd ever eaten, yet he couldn't wait to be finished with supper and go across to the park with a lantern in his hand, where he would propose to Holly under the shining stars.

He looked out of the window, pleased to see that it was snowing gently and softly, in big fat flakes that looked wonderfully Christmassy and romantic.

A hammering on the back door, which led down a small hallway into the servants' hall, made them all jump. Mrs. Goodwin grumbled, "Who can that be?"

"Don't worry, ma'am." Theodore got to his feet. "I'll go and see who it is."

"That's a good boy, Theo." Mrs. Goodwin turned her attention back to her chicken.

Theodore got up, setting down his glass of eggnog, and half wished he hadn't offered to go. The sooner he finished supper, the sooner he could be with Holly. The weight of the ring sagged in his pocket, reminding him with each step that this was about to become the best day of his life as the little iron circlet bumped against his leg.

He was smiling to himself as he opened the door, and his smile grew all the wider when he saw that it was Holly standing there, her hair shining softly in the light from the overhead gas lamp.

"Holly!" he cried. "How lovely to—" His words froze on his lips.

Holly's face was streaked with tears, and utterly ashen. Her chest heaved with running; her bonnet was gone, and her black hair spilled over her shoulders, wild and windblown.

"Holly, what happened?" Theodore reached for her, wrapping his hands around her shoulders. "What's happened?" He thought of Mr. Mills with his cruel, wandering eyes, and a terrible fear gripped his very soul.

Holly stepped back, pulling out of his grip, and gasped his hands in both of hers. Her fingers were shaking uncontrollably, and she was terribly cold. "Theo, you have to go. You have to run."

Theodore's heart froze within him. "Run? Holly, what do you mean? Come inside, where it's warm. You're very frightened."

"There's no time. Mr. Mills has already sent for the police. They'll be here any minute now." A sob shattered Holly's words. "Please. You have to run."

"I... I don't understand." Theodore stared at her. "I've done nothing wrong."

"No... but I have. I've done something terrible... terrible... terrible." Holly let out a ripping sob, and both her hands went to her mouth. "Oh, Theo, Theo, I didn't know. I... I was a fool... I'm a fool. I'm a stupid, stupid fool, and I hope you never see me again."

The ring weighed heavy in his pocket. Theodore felt his heart split apart. "Holly! What are you talking about?"

She covered her face with her hands for a few moments and took a long, shaky breath. When she let her hands fall to her sides, the tears were still coming, but her voice was flat and calm.

"Mr. Mills believes you stole Caroline's necklace. The police are coming, and they'll hang you."

Theodore's heart skipped a beat. Hanging! But relief, too, spread through him. Holly still loved him; she was trying to keep him safe.

"Oh, but Holly, it's all a silly mistake," he said. "I didn't. He's just being a suspicious old man. Why would he think that?"

Holly squeezed her eyes tight shut, her face twisting in pain. "Because I told him I saw you do it."

Theodore felt his world crack. He could only stare at her as she covered her face and sobbed. "Why?" he croaked out.

"I didn't... I... I... I don't know... I was afraid... I was so afraid," Holly sobbed. "I'm such a heartless, heartless fool. Oh, Theo, I'm so sorry. I'm so sorry, but you have to go. You have to run, now, before they get here, before they take you, before..."

Theodore had seen a man hang before. Who hadn't, in this day and age? He remembered the colour of his face. The kicking of his legs over the air. Terror gripped him, a shadow falling over his soul.

"Please, Theo, you have to go," Holly wept. "You have to go. I can hear hoofbeats on the road. They're coming!"

"Holly..." he whispered.

She turned away from him, a hand held out, and the coldness in her voice frightened him even more than the thought of hanging.

"Just go," she moaned.

Then Theodore heard the hoofbeats himself, and the shouts, and the ringing of policemen's bells. There was no time. He reached into his pocket and felt the iron ring, and then Holly was already away, fleeing across the garden back towards the Mills' home.

There was nothing else to do. Theodore looked back once at the kitchen where he had known love and kinship for the first time in his young life. Then, without saying goodbye, he closed the door softly behind him and ran into the dark garden, scaling the back wall with a scrambling leap, and bolting into the darkness of the streets.

* * * *

Holly waited until the house grew silent around her.

Her room was mostly dark, but a comforting sliver of light fell through the window from the gas lamp that burned near it on the outside. She lay on her side in her hard, narrow bed, staring at the scrap of light that shone on the hardwood floor. So many nights she had lain here, looking at that light, dreaming of Theodore as he slept just two houses away. He was something she leaned on in the cold, dark nights, a safe place for her feet to stand.

But now he was there no longer, and when she tried to lean upon the thought of him, she reeled. Heaven only knew where he was; for all she knew, he had already been hanged. The thought made her close her eyes and press her face into the pillow, darkness seeping out of the crack in her heart and spreading through her body like poison.

She had done this to him. She could not erase the image of his face from her mind when she had told him what she had done. Every vestige of colour had drained from his skin. He had been so shocked, so appalled that she could do such a thing.

How could she have done this? She squeezed her pillow into her face, straw pressing through the fabric to tickle her skin. The darkness would never leave her now.

It was part of her now. She was the darkness that she had feared all of her life, and no matter how the Christmas candles shone and the decorations twinkled through the house and the city and the world, it would never reach inside her again.

The housekeeper was snoring in her room next door, and the house had been still for a very long time now. It was time to go.

Holly sat up. She was wearing her green dress — it was the only clothing she owned. Her uniforms were neatly folded in her trunk; she would not take them.

All she took was the same laundry bag she had brought here when she had left Peggy's cottage—oh, how she wished Peggy had never left! It contained just a spare shawl and a pressed flower Theodore had once given her. She slipped on her shoes and moved out of the room without looking back.

Leaving the house was not difficult. The kitchen door was never locked, because of the mastiff that lay by it on guard. The mastiff knew her well. When she slipped through the door, he raised his head and his tail slapped against the floor once or twice before he went back to sleep in his kennel.

Holly did not look back at the Mills' home as she stepped through the garden gate and latched it quietly behind her. She did not look up at the decorations in the homes and gardens all around her as she walked down the street. But when she reached the very end of the street, she did take the pressed flower out of her bag and give it one last, longing look.

A lonely tear slid down her cheek, warm in the frigid air that was already beginning to burn her nose and fingers. She looked at the pressed rose in her palm for a few moments more before closing her fist over it, crushing it to dust. When she opened her hand, the wind caught it and blew it away across the snowy city.

Holly walked away. It was the coldest Christmas Eve she could remember.

Part Four

Chapter Eleven

Two Years Later

Holly stood on the corner of the market square, tucking her bare fingers underneath her armpits in the hopes of shielding them from the bitter wind that howled down the street and tore at the tattered hem of what had once been her good green dress.

She swallowed a few times, praying that her voice would still work despite the raw burning at the back of her throat.

Despite the cold wind, the square swarmed with people. Snatches of laughter burst from the crowd here and there. Everyone was dressed brightly, muffed in furs and thick, knitted scarves; there were not many ragamuffins on these streets, which were even more prosperous than the area where Caroline had lived, just a mile to the south.

A family hurried past Holly, laden with parcels, wrapped in brown paper.

The smallest child brought up the rear, one hand clutching her older sister's skirt, the other holding a spool of ribbon that was just beginning to unroll so that the satiny end of the ribbon flickered in the wind. The child watched it as she walked, her eyes wide with wonder.

Christmas must be very soon.

Holly pushed the thought aside. She knew there was a Christmas tree at the centre of the square, all dusted in snow, with wreaths and ribbons wrapped around its length.

She did not look up at it. Instead, she cleared her throat, ignoring the burning, and wondered if she could get away with singing ordinary songs today.

Perhaps it was worth a try; then again, if she earned no pennies today, it would be her third day in a row without eating. She could sing "Silent Night". At least the word *Christmas* could not be found in that particular carol.

When she opened her mouth, though, the sound would not come. Instead, she sang "Greensleeves", and the crowd barely noticed.

One or two children looked up at her, then hurried after their parents.

Holly knew her voice was not the problem. It had a little gravelly note to it, as it always did in winter, but the sound of it usually could still captivate the attention of anyone walking past.

She pressed it a little harder as she sang the last chorus, holding out her tin cup for coins.

A man stopped, reached into his pocket, then hesitated. Looking up at her face, he gave her a small smile. "Come on, dear," he said. "It's the day before Christmas Eve. Can't you sing us a carol?"

Holly stared at him. The day before Christmas Eve! For Holly, Christmas Eve was the worst, the saddest, the most terrible day of the year. Her eyes filled up and she blinked away the tears.

Her inclination was to say 'no' to the man, she couldn't sing a carol, but her belly burned with hunger, and she could feel the dreaded tremble of weakness in her limbs.

"Yes, sir," she whispered. Clearing her throat again, she began to sing. "Silent night, holy night. All is calm, all is bright."

At least the carol was short. As she sang, she looked into the eyes of the man watching.

A little knot of people gathered around him, listening, and the more Holly sang, the more their eyes softened and smiles spread over their faces.

They were filled with the one thing Holly knew she would never feel within herself again: light.

She reached the end of the song, and there was a scatter of applause from the people gathered, but only two of them bothered to put anything in her cup.

She looked down into it, rattling it in disappointment as the people walked away. A whole day's singing. All she had to show for it was one tuppence and one penny.

It would buy some bread. Holly looked up at the crowd, hesitating. She needed more than bread; she needed a new blanket, and this was a good time of year for singing.

If she could just do a few more carols, people's hearts, softened by the light which she would never feel again, would open just enough to add a few more pennies to her cup.

Carols. She would have to sing more carols.

Sickened, Holly scooped the coins out of the cup and tucked them into her laundry bag, then swung it over her shoulder and trudged down the nearest side street. How could she sing of heavenly peace when she knew she could never deserve it? How could she even say the word "Hallelujah" after what she had done?

She was a fraud, a fool, and a thief for taking this money for singing those words. Words which would never be true for her after she had told such an appalling lie, a lie that could have killed the only man she loved.

The fact that it had not killed him, after all, gave her little comfort. It still could have.

Holly paused only by the bakery to buy a loaf of stable bread before heading down the street, ignoring the baker's cry of "Merry Christmas!" She kept her eyes upon the cobblestones as she passed by the church that stood on the corner, all lit up with candles, wreaths on all the windows.

She did not want to see them. Instead, she pushed down the nearest alley between a row of small, double-storied buildings, each containing a flat above and below.

Squeezing through a gap between rubbish bins, she reached the end of the alley, where a stack of old barrels guarded one corner.

Holly grasped the nearest barrel and hauled it aside to reveal her home. She had built it out of old wooden boxes: a tiny shelter, just big enough for her to sit up in. Newspapers lined the floor, and her threadbare blanket was rolled up in one corner.

She set the laundry bag down beside the blanket and sat down in her shelter, rubbing her hands together. When she could feel her fingers, she broke a piece off the bread and chewed on it.

It was stale and very dry. She kept her eyes up, on the window of the flat beside this alleyway, the upstairs one. It was still dark and silent.

Theodore had not yet come home.

***

Theodore tucked the end of his scarf down the front of his thick woollen jacket as he looked through the big window. Outside, the wind snatched at the wreath hanging over the window, making it swing and bump against the glass.

"It's a bitter wind today, sir," he said, pulling his hat down over his ears.

Mr. Bancroft was busy putting away the last of his books and papers beside his vast desk. "You're quite right, Mr. Smith," he said. "Any special plans for Christmas?"

Theodore slipped his hand into his pocket, out of long habit, and caressed the iron ring that lay there.

It was worn smooth on the outside from the pressure of his fingers over the past two years, but the inside was untouched, and it had never been worn. Some days he hardly knew why he carried it at all. "Just a peaceful evening at home alone, sir," he said.

Mr. Bancroft gave him a speculative look. "You know, Mr. Smith, I'm sure the wife wouldn't object if you were to come tomorrow for Christmas Eve supper."

"Oh, no, sir. I couldn't possibly intrude. What would a lowly worker like me want at the Christmas Eve dinner of a successful businessman like you?"

Mr. Bancroft laughed softly. He walked up beside Theodore, and they watched the whipping wind together. The business opposite theirs had already closed for Christmas, and they had painted the words "MERRY CHRISTMAS AND A HAPPY NEW YEAR!" over their windows.

"You're not a lowly worker anymore, Theodore," said Mr. Bancroft, who rarely used first names for anyone. "You may have been so when you first came to work for the *Chronicle* almost two years ago now, but you're a typesetter now, a skilled tradesman, and you'll work your way still higher." He laid a hand on Theodore's shoulder. "I was a typesetter too, many years ago, and look where I am now."

"That's kind of you, sir."

"No, son, it's smart of *you*. You would still be sweeping the floors and taking out the rubbish if it wasn't for the fact that, unlike most workhouse students, you worked hard and paid attention in your lessons." Mr. Bancroft raised an eyebrow. "In fact, maybe you'll even be a writer one day."

"A writer!" Theodore's lips curled. "Now that would be something."

"Nothing is impossible, my boy." Mr. Bancroft squeezed his shoulder. "And regardless of all that, you know that there will always be a place for you at the Bancroft table after what you did for me that spring."

Theodore shuddered at the mention of that dreadful season. He had been on the streets for three months then, and he had been half dead with illness, half mad with fear, and half starved to boot. "Sir, you're the one who saved *me* that day."

"On the contrary, my boy, I was dead but for you." Mr. Bancroft shook his head. "I suppose I should have known better than to go walking in that slummy district with my gold pocket-watch chain hanging out and my best cigar case in my pocket, but those muggers were brutal. Why, after they'd thrown me to the ground and begun to kick me, and when one of them picked up that bit of broken glass as a knife... I was sure that I was dead."

Theodore shook his head. "The way they mistreated you was awful, sir. I couldn't believe it when I saw them kicking you while you were down."

"Well, I thought perhaps I was being attacked by some kind of demon when you came out of that alley all wild-eyed and shrieking and swinging that plank like a club." Mr. Bancroft chuckled. "The muggers certainly thought so. They turned tail and fled. The last thing I remember before it all went dark was you crouching beside me, saying, 'Don't worry, sir. I'll take care of you'. You were so skin and bones, to this day I don't know how you were able to carry me to the doctor's."

"I'm just happy you still had your cigar case, sir. Otherwise, without your name and address engraved on it, we would never have been able to get you home."

Mr. Bancroft's reminiscent smile was soft. "That's why you'll always be welcome in our home, Theodore. Typesetter or sweeper or journalist or king—whatever you are, you saved my life when you yourself were afraid, when you yourself had nothing. I will always have respect for that."

Embarrassed, Theodore ducked his head. "It's kind of you to say, sir, but my life is already so much more wonderful than I ever imagined it would be." He slipped his hand into his pocket again, thinking that that was very true, except for one thing. "I'm quite happy in my flat."

"Suit yourself, then, Mr. Smith." Mr. Bancroft rose to his feet and donned his hat. "And merry Christmas!"

"Merry Christmas to you, too, sir." Theodore smiled.

He left the office and made his way briskly towards home as the wind whipped and tugged at his scarf and hair. He would buy a piece of fruitcake from the bakery on the corner, and some hot food from the vendor in the market square by the Christmas tree, and then he would go home and stay there peacefully and read some books.

Books! They were his favourite part of his new life. He had enough money to buy them, and his reading was getting better and better now.

He wanted to read all the books in the world, all the ones he had never had the chance to read as a little boy.

When he reached the row of narrow, double-storied buildings that held his flat, his downstairs neighbour was outside, hanging a shiny new wreath on his door. The man was kindly and portly, and he smiled as Theodore came up to him. "Merry Christmas, young man!"

"Merry Christmas, sir!" Theodore smiled back. "Do you need anything?"

"Not at all, lad. You have yourself a nice evening now, and a lovely Christmas Eve tomorrow."

"Thank you very much." Theodore hesitated. "You know, Henry, this is my first Christmas in this area, and I'm wondering if you could point me in the right direction."

"Of course, lad. What can I do for you?"

"I was wondering where I could hear some Christmas carols." Theodore smiled. "I haven't had the chance to listen to carols, apart from church, for a long time, and I have very fond memories of standing in the streets and listening to a choir singing." His heart squeezed again, and he felt the weight of that ring in his pocket, the ring that had seemed to grow heavier and heavier with every month that passed without Holly. He could hardly believe that this would be his second Christmas without seeing her. The mingled pain and anger he had felt on that terrible Christmas Eve, almost exactly two years ago now, was still there; but it was overlaid by an endless, throbbing sense of longing.

"Haven't you heard the girl that sings in the market square?" asked the neighbour, baffled.

"Which square? The nearest one?"

"Aye, that's right. There's a girl sings there almost every day. Pretty, too. Lovely voice. She was singing 'Silent Night' earlier this afternoon."

"That's so strange." Theodore laughed, shaking his head. "I've never seen her, and I go to that square all the time." He remembered hearing a few snatches of singing there several times, and looking around for the singer, but never seeing them.

"I'm sure she'll be singing there tomorrow, poor mite. She's all ragged, like. Reckon she lives on the streets somewhere. Christmas is a good time for her to earn a few pennies." Henry shrugged. "Perhaps you'll see her then, Mr. Smith."

"I'll be sure to go looking for her." Theodore had a spare half-a-crown in the bottom of his drawer; he could take that for the ragged caroller. "Thank you very much, Henry."

He went upstairs to his own little flat. It wasn't much; just a sitting-room, a small bedroom and bathroom, and a tiny kitchenette where he could make tea and sandwiches. His landlady brought his meals up for a small weekly fee. She would bring supper in about an hour.

Theodore pulled off his jacket and poked the fire in the hearth back to life. Then he stood by the window, staring out at the city below, at the lights shining on the streets and the muffled figures of people hurrying past, laden with Christmas shopping and bundled up against the wind. His was the only door on the whole street that did not sport a bright wreath. He admired the decorations everyone else had, but it just didn't seem to be Christmas without Holly.

Sitting down by the fire, he put his hand in his pocket and gently felt for the ring. *Oh, Holly. How will I ever find you again?*

* * * *

Theodore was home.

Holly sat at the edge of her little hideout, knowing that it was too dark for Theodore to see her even if he happened to look out of the window and straight down into the tiny alleyway behind his home.

He never really looked out of this window; in fact Holly seldom saw him except when he sat down to meals at a table just within sight. She could see his gas lamp burning though, and sometimes his shadow upon the wall, or distantly hear him singing to himself.

Now, she heard the clump of footsteps on the stairs leading up to his flat. With the windows closed, Holly couldn't hear words, only the distant rumble of conversation.

His landlady had just brought his supper up to him. She sat up, leaning eagerly out of her shelter. She was about to see him.

He stepped in front of the window, his plate in his hands, and sat down at the table, the gas lamp shining softly on his dark curls. He had had them trimmed in the autumn, but Holly liked them best the way they were now; a loose tousle, messy as when he was just an assistant gardener in the Clifford's' household.

He had some kind of important job now, she knew, at a newspaper. She had never been able to read much—if only she had paid attention in her lessons! Then she could have written to Peggy.

But while she could not write she did know the shape of some words, and she knew the shape of Theo's name.

It was by a kind stroke of luck that she saw his image in a paper one day, right there next to the name Theodore.

Holly was unable to read the story for herself, so she had begged a lady to read her the story in exchange for a song, and Holly had learned about a courageous typesetter who had assisted a woman who had been attacked by a scoundrel.

He had chased the thief down until the woman's valise was retrieved. The man worked for the *Chronicle* and was one of their own, and was called Theodore Smith, so the paper said.

It had taken her weeks to gain the courage to find her way to the *Chronicle* building, hoping against hope that it really was *her* Theodore Bunton.

When she had found him, she had followed him home that night, a few weeks ago now, and prayed for the strength to speak to him.

Of course, she knew she didn't deserve to be near him. All she wanted was to apologize for what she had done, as if that could somehow absolve her guilt.

But the courage had never come to her, so she watched him instead from her shelter as he tucked into a hearty meal, sipping from a mug of hot sweet tea.

No one ever came to visit him in his flat, and she had never seen him with a woman. Perhaps it would have been easier to walk away if she had. But he seemed happy enough, and he wore good warm clothes and had a bright rose in each cheek, and that was enough for Holly.

He deserved all the joy he could find. All the joy of which Holly Gray would never consider herself worthy.

Chapter Twelve

Christmas Eve. 1870

Theodore held the two books in his hands, turning them this way and that, trying to decide which one to buy for Mrs. Bancroft. He had been trying to find a suitable Christmas gift for her all week, but it was difficult to see what a lowly typesetter could buy for a wealthy woman like her.

He knew it was providence when he saw these books in the window of the shop at a special price. They were older novels, and he could see that their corners were well-thumbed, but just the other day Mr. Bancroft had been saying how he couldn't find a copy of George Meredith's *The Adventures of Harry Richmond* anywhere, and how his wife loved the author.

On the other hand… Theodore sighed to himself, glancing at the other book. He knew that Mrs. Bancroft had greatly admired Benjamin Disraeli when he was Prime Minister, and his novel, *Lothair*, was right there in his hands. Which one?

"Last-minute Christmas shopping?" asked Mrs. Hawthorne, the owner of the bookshop, who had been pottering around for the past few minutes, sweeping the floor and preparing to close.

Theodore turned, smiling at the old widow. "Am I keeping you?"

"Oh, dear boy, for you I'd keep this shop open all day." Mrs. Hawthorne chuckled deep in her chest. "It was you, after all, who retrieved my days takings from that scoundrel just a few months ago."

Theodore looked to the floor and gave a small nod. "Help me choose, Mrs. Hawthorne." He laid the books down on the counter. "Which one do you think Mrs. Bancroft will enjoy the most?"

"Ah, I thought you must be shopping for her. Your taste is normally a little more adventurous." Mrs. Hawthorne smiled. "I think she would enjoy both, and you can have them both for the price of one."

"Oh, I couldn't."

"Of course you could, and you shall." Mrs. Hawthorne took a roll of brown paper out from under the counter and wrapped up the books in a parcel, tying them with string. She refused to keep the change, counting out every penny, and pressed it into Theodore's hand. "You have a wonderful Christmas now, my boy."

"Thank you, Mrs. Hawthorne." Theodore smiled widely.

He left the shop with the parcel tucked snugly under his arm. He would send a messenger to the Bancroft's' home with the parcel; he didn't want to intrude on their Christmas Eve celebrations. Though it was early afternoon, the sky pressed down upon the city, low and grey, swallowing up the spire of the church.

Theodore hesitated at the crossroads, standing close to a streetlamp; the pavement was filled with last-minute shoppers like him, and people streamed past him. He'd been up to the market square earlier, hoping to see the singer that Henry had described, and as he walked into the square he thought he heard the distant sound of a beautiful, feminine voice singing. But it had stopped abruptly, and when he reached the square, he saw only the back of a raggedy dress disappearing into the crowd.

Maybe he'd see her if he went back now. His luck had to turn eventually. But it was so cold, and he knew it would snow before nightfall. Better to get home into the warm and curl up in his armchair with a book of his own.

Theodore turned to the right, ready to go back to his flat, and that was when he saw Caroline Mills standing on the pavement behind him.

His body froze, springing tight with the dreadful memory of the night he had been forced to flee the Clifford home because of this girl's lies. No. Surely, surely this was an apparition of his imagination.

But it was her, standing before him in the flesh, wearing a thick fur coat and a grey wool scarf. Her sparkling blue eyes were very wide and fixed on his face, and for a few seconds, neither of them moved nor spoke.

Terror washed through Theodore. Ever since the day he had been accused of theft, he had lived in fear that he would be discovered. That Theodore Bunton was the one who stood accused of stealing Caroline Mills' necklace. His face drained of colour. It seemed that his doom was at the door. Caroline could identify him. Caroline could kill him.

He turned, his eyes searching for the quickest way to flee through the thick cloud and the throng of people, his heart hammering deafeningly in his ears, but before he could break into a run Caroline was beside him with a hand on his arm. He flinched from her touch as though her hand was acid, but it was unexpectedly gentle.

"Mr. Bunton! Theodore. Please, don't run. I'm not going to harm you. I promise," Caroline cried.

Theodore saw his gap and his muscles coiled for flight, but something in Caroline's voice compelled him to stop. He looked at her, and her blue eyes were filling with pleading tears, her hands clasped in front of her.

"Please. Please, don't run away, I beg of you," Caroline sobbed. "Don't take away my only chance to put things right."

Theodore blinked. Had he heard right? He took a wary step back, but did not bolt. "What do you mean?"

"I have been haunted by what I did for months and months," Caroline whispered. The tears spilled over, and they were very different from the great false tears she had cried the day her necklace had been 'lost'.

These tears that flowed now made her nose and eyes burn red, and she was fighting back the sobs with all of her might.

"Please. I have to make things right as much as I can, and if you run away now, I shall never have that chance. I will live forever with the intolerable burden of what I did to you and to poor, sweet Holly."

Theodore hadn't heard Holly's name spoken aloud in years. The sound of it was blissful and shockingly painful. He swallowed hard, trying to fight back his aching heart, which felt as though it would crawl up his chest and strangle him to death.

"You would have killed me," he said.

Caroline hung her head, her voice broken by tears. "Theodore... I... I didn't know. I can't make excuses for what I've done. I was selfish and jealous, and because I was miserable, I couldn't stand to see you and Holly so happy together. I wanted to send you away. I wanted the Clifford's to dismiss you, or for Papa to dismiss Holly, just so that I didn't have to see you anymore... oh, I was so selfish. Oh, Theodore, I was so heartless." She covered her face with her hands and sobbed into them.

Theodore waited. A cold, cold corner of his heart longed to run away from her and never see her again, but the rest of him heard the penitence in her voice and waited, listening.

"But you must believe me when I tell you that I never meant for anyone to be killed." She lowered her hands and looked up at him, her powder streaked across her face with tears. "I didn't know that stealing a necklace would get you hanged. I would never have done it if I had known... but perhaps it was the Lord's grace that I didn't, because in the instant that Papa said you would hang for this, I changed. I realized with a terrible shock what I had done. Yet still I left my necklace hidden, too scared to tell Papa that I had lied. But the next day, I was so scared for you I confessed, so that Papa would stop the police from searching for you. I have suffered greatly for it. Nothing has been the same at home since."

Theodore was beginning to see the real repentance in her. He unfolded his arms. "What happened to Holly?"

"Holly is not working for us anymore." Caroline hung her head. She disappeared the same Christmas Eve that you did." Caroline wiped at her eyes. "Oh, Theodore, I'm so relieved that you're safe. I became dreadfully depressed after what happened. Lonely and hateful. I hated myself. I still do. The only thing I could think to do was to make it my mission to bring you and Holly back together, and I've been searching for you both for more than a year. It was a wonderful thing when I saw an article with your image in the paper about how you helped a woman and retrieved her stolen reticule from a thief outside the *Chronicle* earlier this winter. They said you were called Theo Smith, but I knew it was you."

Theo nodded, but felt no need to explain that he had given himself a different name for fear of the police. And it was just as well because the *Chronicle* had reported the article about the scoundrel who had taken Mrs. Hawthorne's money. Moreover they had placed his image in the paper, proudly, because he was one of the *Chronicles* own. For a while the fear of discovery had become all too real again.

As the meaning of Caroline's words began to sink into Theo's consciousness, relief washed through him. And despite himself, he began to smile and laugh.

"I came to the *Chronicle*," Caroline continued, "but I was too shy to ask after you. I saw that you were well. I thought I would leave you to it, and go to find Holly, and then I did." Caroline paused.

"You know where Holly is?" Theodore laughed out louder, and took a step forward, his heart leaping.

"I do. And I can take you to her."

Theodore's heart jumped into his mouth. He reached into his pocket and felt for the ring, when his heart sunk and a pang of agony ran through him. Holly was the person he loved more than anything, but she had betrayed him. She, too, had almost gotten him killed.

He hesitated, and Caroline saw his hesitation. She stepped forward, grasping his arm.

"Theodore, I know that Holly lied about you, but you must know that I forced her to do it," she murmured. "And more than anything, you must know that she loves you. She has always loved you. She will never stop. Please… you must give her another chance."

Theodore suddenly wasn't sure that he could. But he nodded, and Caroline led him towards the market square, turning down a narrow alley. "We must sneak into the square," she whispered. "Holly would bolt if she saw me."

"She's in this square?" Theodore asked as they slipped into a small, walled-off courtyard behind one of the shops. He was fairly sure that they were trespassing, and it made his skin crawl.

"Yes, she must be." Caroline paused. "I think she is."

"But I come to this square all the time... for my shopping."

"She flees when she sees you. It's as though she's always keeping a watch for you, to make sure you won't see her." Caroline stopped in her tracks. "There! Can you hear her?"

Theodore wasn't sure what he was meant to be listening for, but a moment later, he heard it, loud and clear and close by. It was the feminine voice, and once again, it was singing "Silent Night". The voice was far more hoarse than he remembered Holly's being, but now that he was close enough to hear it clearly, he knew it was hers.

"Silent night, holy night. All is calm, all is bright..."

Theodore rushed up to the nearest wall of the courtyard and pulled himself up to look over the top, resting his elbows on the wall, and she was standing on the corner furthest from the Christmas tree. One hand was pressed to her heart as she sang, and the words floated around the square like magic.

"... round yon Virgin Mother and Child," Holly sang. Her hair was matted and unruly in the dull, distant sunlight, and her cheeks were as thin and pale as they had been in the workhouse. The tattered remnants of her green dress clung pathetically to her withered frame. "Holy Infant so tender and mild. Sleep in heavenly peace... sleep in heavenly peace."

As she sang the last note, her eyes, constantly scanning the square, found Theodore's face. For a second, their gaze locked. The crowd was applauding. Holly did not seem to hear them. Instead, when she saw him, her eyes widened, and she froze like a frightened animal.

Something rushed through Theodore's body, something warm and glorious and certain. A tide of wild love, love that kept no record of wrongs, love that was patient and kind, and it drove him over the wall before he knew what he was doing.

"Holly!" Her name burst free from his lips like a bird taking wing.

She let out a sob, grabbed her skirts, turned tail and bolted.

"Holly, no!" Theodore cried. He rushed forward, but already she was pushing through the crowd, threatening to disappear among the Christmas shoppers. "Holly!" he cried, trying to follow her, but the crowd was so thick. "Holly!"

He caught a final glimpse of her black hair disappearing into the crowd, but when he pushed through them to the same spot, she was gone; vanished into the maze of alleyways surrounding the market square. Theodore's heart throbbed within him. How could she be gone? He turned this way, then that, but there was no sign of her. Finding her would be impossible in the chaos of side streets here.

He turned, looking for Caroline, but she, too, had disappeared. Even surrounded by a crowd of people, Theodore had never before felt so achingly alone.

It was at that moment that it began to snow. Great, fat, shimmering white flakes, just like the night that his world had been torn apart.

* * * *

Holly's heart pounded wildly in her ears, driving her on. She burst through the crowd, reaching the far side of the market square, and risked a single glance back over her shoulder.

Theodore cried her name again. She could just see him pushing through the crowd some distance away, and the sight of him made her feel as though she was being torn in two. Oh, how she longed to run to him! Oh, how she longed to feel his arms around her one more time! But she couldn't be near him, not after what she had done, and so she turned and redoubled her pace, taking a sharp turn down an alleyway to her left.

The turn was too sharp. Her shabby, worn shoes caught a patch of ice and her feet shot out from under her.

With a cry of alarm, Holly threw out an arm, trying to catch herself, and heard a sickening crunch somewhere in her wrist as her palm slammed against the cobblestones. Her arm gave way, and she fell heavily, her shoulder and hip crashing against the stone with numbing agony. It was all she could do to stop her head from striking the ground.

"Holly!"

Theodore was still after her. She scrabbled to her hands and knees and dragged herself just far enough down the alley that she could hide behind a stack of old barrels, her breath and heart racing, terrible pain stinging through her cold wrist.

With all her strength, Holly forced herself not to cry out. She bit down on her lip and huddled among the barrels, listening to Theodore's breathless voice call her name another time or two.

Please give up, she whispered to him in her soul. *Please go away*.

She longed with everything in her to rise and run to him, but what if he rejected her?

Worse, what if he forgave her, and she would have to live knowing that she had wounded the best man she had ever known?

At last, she heard his footsteps taking him away, and she dragged herself to her feet.

It was cold here. She needed to go back to her shelter, curl up there and hope that time would heal whatever was so badly harmed in her wrist. She could hardly care. All she wanted was to sleep and forget her misery for a few brief hours.

Taking the first step down the alley, Holly had to bite back a scream of sheer agony as her wrist panged horrifically, a strange crunching sound coming from it.

She braced it with her other arm as well as she could and limped down the street, noting dully that it was snowing. Soon it would be even colder and even harder to move through these streets.

She would have to find another place to sing… uproot her life all over again… give up her glimpses of Theodore. The thought made her want to collapse in a heap and wait on the cold stone for the winter to take her life as it had taken so many others on the streets of London.

Something deep inside prodded her to keep going. Somehow, she wandered on, back towards her shelter.

Every step was jarring agony; every moment made her breath catch, made her tremble with pain. The distance seemed to have multiplied by ten since she had come this way that same morning.

Rest... she needed a rest. She felt she was unable to take another step, not with her arm paining her so dreadfully. Looking up, Holly realized she was standing in front of the church on the corner.

She had passed it by so many times, keeping her head down to avoid looking at it and its decorations and the light that poured out from within, that she had never noticed that the door was always open. Even now, with the snow blowing on the wind, the door stood open a crack.

She stared at it dully for a few moments. Part of her wanted nothing to do with this church, yet she could see the inviting pews within, a place to rest out of the cold.

Even though she felt she would besmirch the place with her very presence within it, she dared not brave the cold with her aching arm for a moment longer. She would sit down just for a few moments, and rest, and then she would go back to her shelter.

Slowly, wincing at each step, with tears of pain running down her cheeks, Holly stumbled her way into the church. She sank down into one of the pews, hugging her arm to her chest. It felt so good to sit on something that was actually meant for sitting, instead of on the floor or on a broken old box.

She leaned back, taking deep breaths, keeping her eyes closed so that she would not look up at the altar or the decorations that hung everywhere or the candles burning so brightly in their niches, reminding her that her very presence in this holy place was a desecration. What did it matter? There was no hope for her in any case.

She thought of the way Theodore had called her name. There had been love and hope in his voice, she was sure of it. He had wanted to see her. Perhaps even to forgive her. He was so good to her, and yet she had almost caused his death. A tear splashed on her skirt.

She deserved the refractory ward, the terrible impact of that ruler on her hand, just as Mrs. West had taught her in the workhouse. Punishment for mistakes was the only way she knew.

If only there was some other way, some way to erase everything that she had ever done. If only she could be free of the burden of her sin.

If that was the case, she could run to Theodore's arms, and hold him at last. But it wasn't, and so she knew, with a terrible bone-deep certainty, that she would not survive this Christmas. Not with her aching arm and her empty belly and the snow that pattered softly on the high roof of the church.

"Hello," said a voice beside her. "Are you hurt? Do you need help?"

Holly jumped, the movement sending a lancing pain through her wrist.

She clutched it close and cried out, terrified by the paralyzing pain that spread through her body.

If it had not been for that pain, she would have been on her feet and fleeing out of the church door already; as it was, she was frozen in place, looking up at the tall blond man that stood in the aisle between the pews. He wore a long white vestment, and his golden hair seemed to shine softly on his shoulders. He must be preparing for the Christmas Eve service, although Holly couldn't remember if the priests in the chapel back at the workhouse had worn white vestments quite so soft and fine and clean as this one.

"Don't be afraid," said the man. He sat down on the pew beside her, leaving a space open so that she could still flee, but suddenly she felt she didn't want to. The man reached out and rested a long-fingered hand on her shoulder. "You look hungry and frightened. Are you all right?"

Holly wanted to say yes, she was, and to shuffle out of the pew and get out of the church at once. But somehow the truth was spilling from her. "I'm not all right," she whispered, tears trickling down her cheeks. "I'm hurt, but that's not the worst of it. The worst of it is that it's Christmas and all around me I see light and hope and joy and forgiveness, and love, and I can never have any of it, never, ever again." She clutched both arms more tightly to her chest, feeling the disgusting weight of the darkness within her, crushing and crushing.

"How so?" asked the man.

"I've done something terrible. Something that hurt a friend, that could have killed them." Holly swallowed her tears. "I feel broken and filthy, and I wish I could have just a little piece of the light and hope of Christmas, but I know I can't. It'll never be mine again."

"Oh, child." The man squeezed her shoulder very softly. "Don't you know that we all have darkness inside us?"

Holly stared up at him. How had he known about the darkness?

"There's not one of us that's pure or perfect, not one," said the man, "yet Christmas belongs to us all."

"Even to me?" Holly whispered.

"Especially to you, child." The man smiled. "Christmas, and its hope, joy, and light, belongs to anyone who will reach out their hands and accept its free gift."

At last, Holly permitted herself to look up at the altar and the candles blazing upon it, and a sudden hope jumped in her. Could the darkness fade? Could she allow the light to come flooding in? She closed her eyes, tears burning, and longed for joy and hope to come back to her, and somehow it did. Somehow she felt new strength flow into her, despite the hunger that still gnawed at her and the terrible pain in her arm.

Holly rose to her feet. "I have to go," she said.

The man stared at her. "Do you need help? You look hurt."

"No, I have to go," she said again, and turned and went back out of the doors as quickly as her arm would allow, feeling as though she weighed a thousand times less, as though the light of every candle in every window in London had suddenly entered her heart.

She had already reached the garden gate by the time she realized that she hadn't thanked the kind man in white. She stopped and looked back, but he had already gone.

* * * *

The snow burned on Holly's skin with each new flake that blew against her, buffeted by a cruel wind that seemed to take special pleasure in plucking at her wounded arm. A fresh burst of pain forced her to a halt, and she stood on a street corner, teeth gritted, wheezing with effort and agony as she waited for the spasm to pass.

It wasn't much further now. She prayed with all of her heart for the strength to reach her destination.

Taking a deep breath, she took another step forward, and another. Around her, the city had grown quiet. Everyone was snugly indoors, behind the bunting on the windows and the wreaths on the doors, celebrating together. Everyone except for a thin girl in a ragged dress struggling against the wind and snow.

She had long wondered why Theodore's door lacked a wreath, but now she felt a great cascade of relief wash over her when she lifted her eyes and saw the bare door just across the street. She stopped, hovering, terrified for an instant that the darkness would come back and the terrible guilt and shame would drive her away.

But it did not. Instead she found herself stepping forward with all the haste she had, her heart thundering in anticipation as she dragged herself up the steps to the undecorated door.

It took all of her courage to hold her injured arm still as she raised the other hand. She could manage only a single, weary knock before clutching her broken arm again. Had he heard? Was he home? A gas light was on in the window. *Please, please, let him be home.*

He was. The door creaked open, and Theodore was standing there in a navy blue suit, his hair rumbled, his feet in stockings, looking at her, and she had never seen anything so glorious in all of her life.

Her numb lips somehow formed the name. "Theodore."

Motion rippled through Theodore's body as though he would snatch her into his arms, but he stopped himself. He was trembling. Not a word escaped him.

Holly took the deepest breath she could. "I'm not asking you to forgive me. I'm just asking you to listen. I want to tell you that I'm sorry for what I did to you. I have no excuses, no reasons. I'm just sorry, Theo. I'm so, so sorry." Tears began to spill from her. "If you can't forgive me, then I'll understand. I just want you to know that I'm so…"

"Oh, Holly!" Theodore gasped. "I forgave you long ago."

And with those world-shattering words, he stepped forward and wrapped his arms around her, very tenderly, and she was drawn safely into his embrace at last.

* * * *

It awed Holly how much her world had changed in a single day.

She was curled up on the sofa in Theodore's small living room, slightly drowsy from the medicine that had effectively dulled the pain in her arm to a gentle ache and the sleep from which she had just woken.

The clean satin slip she wore was a little too big for her, but it was comfortable and soft; she had almost forgotten what it was like to wear something completely clean. The blanket wrapped around her was even cleaner and softer. Her stomach was full, a little uncomfortably so, with all of the roast chicken and fruit cake and chestnuts and oranges she had eaten for Christmas lunch an hour ago.

But best of all, Theodore sat in an armchair just opposite her, staring into the fire despite the book that lay open on his lap.

Holly studied the way the flames leaped on the lines of his face. She could barely believe that she had been stumbling through the streets alone and afraid at this time yesterday, half starved and half frozen to death. Everything had changed since she had come to Theodore's door, collapsing with pain.

Theodore's landlady had rushed in to help—a sweet, lonely old spinster named Miss Clarke.

Miss Clarke had brought her into the cottage and stoked the fire while Theodore went for the doctor. There had been hot drinks and medicine and baths and clean clothes, even if she had had to borrow them from Miss Clarke, a somewhat portly old lady. And she had slept on Theodore's bed, with Miss Clarke acting as chaperone while Theodore slept in his chair.

He was far from falling asleep again now, his eyes intent on the flames. Holly could only wonder what he was thinking. She barely knew what would happen next. Perhaps he'd help her to find work, and she could live in a tenement.

Theodore's eyes flickered to her, and a smile replaced the thoughtful look upon his face. "Holly! You're awake."

He set aside the book and came over to her, kneeling beside the sofa. "How does your arm feel?"

"Much better, thank you." Holly pushed back the blankets and sat up, smoothing down her hair. Her arm was snug in a plaster cast, and she could barely feel it through the medicine the doctor had left for her.

"That's wonderful." Theodore beamed up at her as though she was the most magnificent thing he had ever seen.

Miss Clarke rose from the chair opposite, setting down her knitting. "Something to eat, pet?" she asked.

"Oh, no thank you, Miss Clarke." Holly laughed. "I think I would explode if I ate anything more."

A sound floated to them through the closed window. Miss Clarke tilted her white head a little to one side. "Do I hear carollers?"

"You do indeed, Miss Clarke. Theodore went over to the window and grinned. "They're walking through the back street. All robes and candles. It's lovely."

"Open the window, dear, so that we can hear them," said Miss Clarke.

Theodore flung the window wide, and the words floated into the room, borne upon the high and pure voices of the choir.

"Joy to the world! The Lord is come. Let Earth receive her King!"

Theodore turned to Holly, holding out a hand.

It was a strange thing, to dance like this to a Christmas carol, and Holly hardly had the strength to do anything more than sway. But she leaned her face into Theodore's chest, and Miss Clarke retreated discreetly back to her chair, and nothing else mattered. Not her aching arm, not her tired limbs, not even the chill air blowing in through the window. All that existed was Holly and Theodore and the light that filled her heart to the brim.

The carollers moved on, switching to "O Come All Ye Faithful". Holly looked up into Theodore's gentle eyes, and a smile played over his lips. He gripped both of her hands for a moment, then sank to one knee and reached into his pocket.

"Th-Theodore?" Holly whispered.

Theodore held up a small, iron ring, its outside worn smooth by loving touch, and his eyes held all the Christmas lights in the world.

"Holly Gray, would you marry me?"

Afterwards, Holly was never quite sure what she actually said to him. She only knew that her entire being was reduced to a single, glorious *Yes!*

Epilogue

Holly sat curled up on the sofa next to Theo, a swirl of snowflakes gently falling outside their window, in Theo' arms, their new baby lay sleeping peacefully.

This year, Peggy was visiting with them. *It was a perfect Christmas,* Holly thought. Dear Peggy's consumption had much improved considerably since living in the country. She would never fully recover, but at least for now, she was well. *One day at a time*, Peggy had told them.

Yesterday, on Christmas eve morning, Peggy had cried when they had revealed their baby's name as Margaret Joanna. "Oh, lovey, I never expected that. It's an honour. A real honour. Are you sure you don't want to call her Joanna Margaret?"

"You are the mama Joanna sent me Peggy. And I believe that with all my heart. I know I've said it many times, but thank you for taking a deathly ill child off the streets and caring for her. You were a miracle sent to me by my mama."

With the help of Theo to give her courage, Holly had returned to the workhouse for the records of her mother, and learned Joanna Gray had passed many years before, even before Holly had fled the workhouse.

"Here, now, that's enough cryin'," Peggy had said, wiping the tears from her old eyes. "I'll see to that goose and the pudding, so we're all ready for tomorrow."

And now on this Christmas day, with Peggy and Theo and little Margaret, the deliciousness of Christmas wrapped around the room with the smell of roasting meats, vegetables and the plum pudding, boiling on the stove top. A small tree sat in the corner of the room decorated with oranges, and baubles, an Angel atop the branches. A happy smile played across Holly's lips as she remembered the man dressed in white from the Christmas before.

The man had glowed, it seemed. He had helped her when she had believed Theo could never forgive her, and when she believed she was worth nothing—nothing at all. The man who-ever, what-ever he was, had helped her believe differently.

"I say, whatever did become of that girl Caroline Mills?" Peggy said.

"Theo and I saw her fairly recently, in passing. She mentioned that she has decided to become a nurse. I hope she will find her happiness."

Holly saw no reason to tell Peggy the entirety of what had happened. Holly had no room in her heart for bitterness or regrets.

Every-one deserved a second chance.

She knew that better than anyone and held only gratitude in her heart.

Holly believed in love and forgiveness, and Holly believed in Christmas miracles.

The End.

I hope that you enjoyed this book.

If you are willing to leave a short and honest review for me on Amazon, it will be very much appreciated, as reviews help to get my books noticed.

Receive FREE Books Available only to Subscribers

Subscribe here to receive Nell Harte's newsletter.

Over the page you will find a preview of one of my other books

PREVIEW

The Nurses Plight

Nell Harte

Chapter One

Bath, June 1854

"I can assure you; I would be of little use as a wife. For one thing, I still cannot fathom why there is a difference between the "good" crockery and the everyday. It all holds your dinner the same way."

Diana Bickerstaff thought a jest might hide the tremble in her voice, for she had never been so bold in all her nine-and-ten years upon the Earth. "Please, Father. Would you not take even a morsel of pride in seeing your daughter do something valuable with her life?"

The father in question, Christopher Bickerstaff, paced like a caged beast in front of the fireplace; the dancing flames somewhat indulgent considering the evening was tepid outside.

The firelight cast grim shadows upon his glowering face, silhouetting a monstrous figure across the drawing room ceiling, as if a great raven were stretching its wings out to herald a terrible omen. Diana thought it rather befitting, for her entire future rested upon her father's answer.

Her mother, Lilian, seated daintily upon the settee, clicked her tongue in disapproval and raised her gaze from her painstaking embroidery of a young girl picking daffodils. "Are you trying to imply that being a wife is not a valuable vocation?"

She set her embroidery down, which Diana knew spelled trouble. "Have *I* done nothing with my existence for the five-and-twenty years that I have been married to your father? I suppose you think I should have abandoned you to a nursemaid instead of spending my days raising you properly, or is it only marriage you deem unworthy of you?"

Diana had expected such a retort. Indeed, she had prepared for it, but as her mother struck her with a cold, damning stare, all of the words and rehearsed appeasements vanished from her mind.

Perhaps, I am *asking for too much. Perhaps, I should just do what is expected of me. But why should I? Why should I do something I do not want to?* Diana's thoughts waged a silent battle, flitting between the habits of a lifetime of obedience and the more recent surge of defiance and grand hopes that seemed to want to shape what was *left* of her lifetime.

"For you, it was a worthwhile vocation," Diana replied gingerly, willing her rehearsed script to come back to her. "The world was different when you were my age. Being a nurse was not a viable occupation for ladies, back then, but a woman can now do more than… um… just marry and have children. That is not to say I will never marry, but I know I could do some good in the meantime, Mother. I promise, if you allow me to attend St. John's, I will not disappoint you."

Christopher paused in his pacing and rested his knuckles on his hips, huffing out a sigh as he gazed toward the window, where the sun had shattered into a golden haze: a final burst of beauty before it began to sink slowly into the horizon. "I blame that wretched Nightingale woman, filling the heads of young ladies with nonsense."

Lilian nodded in agreement. "She is perceived as some sort of heroine but, as I understand it—and I have acquaintances who have heard from someone who has met her, so the authority is good—that she is merely an ugly woman who is ill-suited to anything else." She grinned rather cruelly. "Why, according to my friends, she is the living embodiment of *Sairey Gamp.*"

"I always liked that Dickens fellow. A wise man." Christopher chinned toward his daughter. "You would do well to read *Martin Chuzzlewit* again, if you think becoming a nurse is at all respectable. They are drunken fools, shaking so badly from their "Mother's Ruin" that you would not want one near you if you were in need of sutures! Indeed, if you could find one at all, for I hear they are all lying in gutters somewhere, snoring so loudly it could wake the dead. So, perhaps, they are not entirely useless if you desire a resurrection!"

Diana's mother and father both cackled as though something terribly amusing had unfolded, while Diana merely stood there, flanked by the two brocade settees, feeling an angry, embarrassed heat flare in her cheeks.

By mocking Florence Nightingale, they were mocking Diana's hopes and dreams and, indeed, the woman she idolised as a revolutionary heroine to be admired and applauded.

To rub salt into the wound, her mother and father clearly did not care that they were insulting everything she held dear: the great purpose that would steer her future course.

Prior to hearing the name "Florence Nightingale," and before the first thrilling titbits and droplets of information about the brave nurse had been gobbled up, Diana had been somewhat at a loss about her life.

As a young lady of the middle-class, there were expectations, but all they had ever done was fill her with dread. Indeed, the more those expectations barrelled toward her as she matured into womanhood, the more inclined she was to crave something more than marriage and childbearing.

A year ago, *just* at that tipping point on the scale of her life, a friend had mentioned Florence Nightingale to her, and everything had changed. She had found a new sense of clarity, finally seeing a purpose and a direction that would satisfy her, but it had been a long feat of endurance, trying to gather all of the information and possibilities of how to make it her reality.

Now, convincing her mother and father was the final hurdle, and she felt as though she was stumbling badly.

"*Sairey Gamp* is a caricature," Diana grumbled feebly.

Her father snorted. "There is truth in caricature, Diana. Plenty of truth in that particular one; I am sure!"

"It is my belief, and the belief of many young ladies like myself, that Dickens was trying to ridicule the very notion of women being valued, important figures in the realm of medicine," Diana persevered, remembering some of what she had intended to say.

"Yet, if he were injured or unwell, he would not sniff at a nurse offering to ease his suffering. Nor would you, I hope.

Indeed, that is why I wish to learn at St. John's House. It is a respectable establishment, led by Sisters—an ordained sisterhood. You are not suggesting that those who are bound to God could be disreputable, are you?"

Her mother and father looked at her as if she were the worst child in all of England, yet the point remained: they could not say that they deemed the sisterhood to be disreputable without making themselves sounds immoral, but they seemed determined to continue with the belief that nurses were scoundrels and drunks. Diana had hoped it would prove to be a dichotomy for them, challenging their thoughts on the matter.

"Of course not!" Lilian almost choked on her own spittle in outrage. "But you, darling, have not taken religious orders. You are not a nun. You are not part of a sisterhood. Your father and I are obviously speaking of those who are *just* nurses. Why would any woman of our station desire such a... lowly occupation? Indeed, why should you desire any occupation at all, when a fine husband will offer a life of comfort and happiness?"

Because I am bored of "comfort," because I wish to be of use to society, because I would not be what you are, because I do not want to lose who I am, because I am not like you, Diana wished she had the courage to say such things, but just standing there, asking to be allowed to journey to London to gain an education at St. John's House was taking up every shred of bravery she possessed.

"She is trying to gain an audience with Queen Victoria, you know," Diana said instead, hearing the weakness of her argument as she spoke.

Her father raised a bushy eyebrow. "Who? The nuns?"

"Florence Nightingale." Diana chewed the inside of her cheek, staring down at the floor as her cheeks burned more fiercely.

Her mother scoffed. "As if the Queen would allow that. She does not want waifs and strays leaving the stench of gin in her palace."

"It is true!" Diana insisted, driven by her adoration for a woman she had never met. "She wants to journey to Crimea to assist in healing our fine Englishmen on the battlefields. *She* wants to make a change, and so do I. Yet, you would call that sense of valour *lowly*?"

At least her mother and father had the decency to look mildly ashamed of themselves, for no one, not even them, could escape the horrific stories that were filtering out of Crimea and arriving on the sad tides that brought back a never-ending current of wounded soldiers.

As for those who would never come home, the list of lost souls grew ever longer with each snippet of news passed from the docking ships to the rest of the country. It moved like a sluggish plague, breaking hearts and families, robbing mothers of sons and wives of husbands, and sparking a fever in the very body of England, whipping the population into a frenzy of outrage.

In a way, Diana supposed she had caught that fever, though her symptoms were ones of fiery determination. It had made her believe that if the young men could fight and die and suffer for their country, the young women had a duty to do their part, too.

"Soldiers, *our* soldiers, are dying not only on foreign shores, but on their way back to their homeland," Diana went on. "The country is irate. All you need do is open your beloved papers to see that. The people are crying out for more to be done to aid those gallant men, and I would be a small piece of that help if you would just allow me to begin my training."

Her father looked away.

She knew why. Whenever the country was at war, or spoke of war, a haunted expression clouded his face. He had fought in his youth, gaining an injury to his leg that had left a jagged smile from calf to thigh.

The wound had healed, but his pride had not, and the old scar ached in the cold months, his subtle limp worsening as the years grew unkinder towards him.

Soon, he would have to walk with a cane, though Diana knew he would be too stubborn to use one, choosing to struggle for the sake of the pride he had left.

Sooner than you think, Father, you might need a nurse like me. She did not dare to say so out loud.

"If you would but read of Florence in the papers, you might understand." Diana cleared her throat for her last attempt at a rousing persuasion.

"She speaks of the conditions in the country's hospitals, and how atrocious they are. She says you would have to see it to believe it, but she *has* seen it, and she would change it, regardless of the scorn and ridicule she receives. The men who are fortunate enough to escape Crimea with their lives are suffering terribly when they return, but she is trying to improve sanitation and care, encouraging more young ladies to become what she is. I see nothing lowly in that."

For a long while, her parents said nothing, both absent in their own thoughts. Her mother looked remorseful, occasionally trying to catch Christopher's eye, but he stared only at the golden-hued sky, where the pink-tinged clouds floated by so slowly that the entire world looked like an exquisite painting. Celestial shafts of light pierced the clouds, caressing the earth below with heaven's fingertips. Diana hoped it meant her prayers would be answered, for this particular prayer called for a not inconsiderable sum of money.

"You made an intriguing argument, but it is out of the question," her father said, at last, in a quiet blow that was more crushing than a pianoforte being dropped upon Diana's head.

"Why?" was the only thing she could ask.

Her father turned, wearing a look of grim resolve. "I will not allow my only child to embarrass this family, when I have toiled ceaselessly to make it what it is. You think of nursing as courageous, but it is no better than the soot-streaked sweeper who crawls up and down the chimneys." He paused. "What I mean by that is, it is a position for the working class. It is not for the likes of us."

"But St. John's permits ladies from every class," Diana insisted.

"It is a dirty trick, Diana," her father replied firmly. "If it were so noble, this "House" of which you are so enamoured would not ask for any coin from any class. Yet, they ask for *our* class of people to pay so that they may spend that money upon the poor who have been too idle to work for it. If the lowest ranks of society wish to tend to wounded men, let them work for the money to pay for such an education."

Diana floundered for a retort, for she had not prepared for that part of the argument. Indeed, it *was* true that the middle classes had to pay in order to be trained by the sisterhood of St. John's, while the working classes did not, but she was certain there was a good reason for it.

"It is… It is… It is to elevate them!" she blurted out. "It is a way for poor young women to escape poverty. Is that not a righteous thing? Should we not encourage that, when we are in a position of privilege? Should we not want that?"

Her father sneered, as she had suspected he might. "There is no such thing as poverty, just indolence. Any man can *elevate* themselves and their families from nothing if they choose to, but they do not; they choose to imbibe and brawl and cause trouble instead. I will not give my money so that a loafer's daughter can become a nurse and spend her money on gin and goodness knows what else."

His voice carried a firm tone that Diana knew all too well. Each word provided a brick for the invisible walls that were going up around her father, making his heart and mind impenetrable to her pleas.

"It is what I want, Father," Diana said, regardless. Her battle was on the brink of being lost, but she would not surrender entirely.

"And I should like my leg to work as it used to, but we cannot always have what we want," her father shot back. "You will marry a respectable man, become a respectable wife and mother, and live the way every lady before you have done. You say the world has changed, Diana, but I say, why change something that works perfectly well as it is?"

Diana bowed her head. "Very well, Father."

"We shall hear no more of this; do you understand me?"

She nodded. "Yes, Father."

"Now, go and make yourself truly useful, and ask Mrs. Soames to bring us some tea. This unpleasantness has made me rather parched," her father instructed: his expression relaxing. He knew he had won, so confident in his paternal power that he likely believed the conversation was finished forever.

As Diana left the drawing room, however, she knew differently. Her future could not and would not be relinquished so easily, for it was the only thing she had ever wanted, and the only thing she had ever really asked for.

Later that evening, as rain pattered against the windows of the fine country house, cooling the earth after a balmy day that heralded the arrival of true summer, Diana yawned her way down the stairs to bid goodnight to her parents.

She had fallen asleep, book in hand, having worn herself out with frustrated tears in the peace of her bedchamber.

She would have stayed there, in truth, but not bidding goodnight to her mother and father each and every night was deemed as shameful as asking to become a nurse.

Padding softly down the hallway, illuminated by lanterns and candles that flickered in her wake, Diana paused at the hushed sound of voices. Her mother and father seemed to be deep in conversation in the drawing room—so deep that they had not heard the footfalls of their only child.

Curious, Diana tiptoed closer, pressing her back flat to the wall so she would not cast a suspicious shadow and draw their attention. The door was open ajar, allowing her to hear them clearly.

"If we do not do something swiftly, darling, she is going to end up like that sister of yours!" Diana's father hissed. "She bowed her head and agreed to conclude the conversation, but she has become wilful this past year. She must consider me a fool if she thinks I believe she will forget about it. I do not know what change has occurred in her, but we must nip it in the bud before it can grow into wildness. She *must* obey."

Her mother sighed. "I know, my dear." She paused. "I wonder if there is some corruption in the blood, for I fear she has already become like my sister. When Joan was eight-and-ten, she fled a betrothal. We shall have to keep a close eye upon Diana if we do not want her to do the same thing."

Diana clamped a hand over her mouth to stop a gasp from escaping.

All her life, she had been informed that her aunt had married a nice gentleman and had gone to live with him in the north. Diana had met her aunt only once, when she had come to the house, wishing to speak with her sister about something.

But it was so long ago that Diana could not remember how the visit had unfolded, nor could she remember much about her aunt. Still, it was clear, now, that the entire thing had been a lie.

"I will go into town tomorrow and speak with Peter," her father said solemnly. "He has been trying to get me to accept a betrothal between Andrew and Diana since they were children. I suppose I shall have to accept, though I always thought she was charming enough to attract a Lord. Never mind. Andrew shall have to suffice."

A boulder of dread sank slowly from Diana's throat, through her chest, and down into the pit of her stomach. She loathed the young man in question, Andrew Rivers, almost more than any other man she had ever encountered. Arrogant, rude, and sordid in nature, Andrew was the very last person she could ever consider marrying.

If Father does this tomorrow, I am running out of time, she realised, as panic leapt through her in sharp barbs.

Had her parents not pressed her, she might have been content to feign obedience for another year or two, while she conjured a way to make her own money in secret.

Now, they had made her decision for her. She would not play the role of a dutiful daughter, wedding a man she hated in order to keep the peace. If that meant she had to run away, just as her aunt had, then so be it.

As for her education at St. John's House, she could contend with that when she came to it. First, however, she needed to escape the trap that was closing around her and find a way to London without anyone stopping her.

Tonight… It has to be tonight. It was not what she had hoped for, and the prospect of slipping away in the dead of night was not a welcome thought, but no matter what dangers lay out there in the world, they could not be any worse than being the wife of Andrew Rivers.

At least, in her youthful naivety, that was what she believed.

READ THE REST

https://geni.us/NursesPlight

Printed in Great Britain
by Amazon